Kristine Kathryn Rusch is one of the best writers in the field.

—*SFRevu*

Whether [Rusch] writes high fantasy, horror, sf, or contemporary fantasy, I've always been fascinated by her ability to tell a story with that enviable gift of invisible prose. She's one of those very few writers whose style takes me right into the story—the words and pages disappear as the characters and their story swallows me whole….Rusch has style.

—Charles de Lint
The Magazine of Fantasy & Science Fiction

The SF thriller is alive and well, and today's leading practitioner is Kristine Kathryn Rusch.

—*Analog*

Praise for
THE RUNABOUT

[The Runabout] is so good, it will make you want to read the other stories."

—*SFRevu*

"Amazing character construction, building a plot that riveted me almost from the moment it began. I will now absolutely have to read the preceding titles and I cannot wait to see what will come as a result of *The Runabout*."

—*Tangent Online*

Praise for
DIVING INTO THE WRECK

Rusch delivers a page-turning space adventure while contemplating the ethics of scientists and governments working together on future tech.
—*Publisher's Weekly*

This is classic sci-fi, a well-told tale of dangerous exploration. The first-person narration makes the reader an eyewitness to the vast, silent realms of deep space, where even the smallest error will bring disaster. Compellingly human and technically absorbing, the suspense builds to fevered intensity, culminating in an explosive yet plausible conclusion.
—*RT Book Reviews* Top Pick

Rusch's handling of the mystery and adventure is stellar, and the whole tale proves quite entertaining.
—*Booklist Online*

The technicalities in Boss' story are beautifully played…. She's real, flawed, and interesting…. Read the book. It is very good.
—*SFFWorld.com*

Praise for
CITY OF RUINS

Rusch keeps the science accessible, the cultures intriguing, and the characters engaging. For anyone needing to add to their science fiction library, keep an eye out for this.
—Josh Vogt
SpeculativeFictionExaminer.com

Praise for
BONEYARDS

Rusch's latest addition to her "Diving" series features a strong, capable female heroine and a vividly imagined far-future universe. Blending fast-paced action with an exploration of the nature of friendship and the ethics of scientific discoveries, this tale should appeal to Rusch's readers and fans of space opera.

—*Library Journal*

Filled with well-defined characters who confront a variety of ethical and moral dilemmas, Rusch's third Diving Universe novel is classic space opera, with richly detailed worldbuilding and lots of drama.

—*RT Book Reviews*

Praise for
SKIRMISHES

. . . a fabulous outer space thriller that rotates perspective between the divers, the Alliance and to a lesser degree the Empire. Action-packed and filled with twists yet allowing the reader to understand the motives of the key players, *Skirmishes* is another intelligent exciting voyage into the Rusch Diving universe.

—*The Midwest Book Review*

Kristine Kathryn Rusch is best known for her Retrieval Artist series, so maybe you've missed her Diving Universe series. If so, it's high time to remedy that oversight.

—Don Sakers, *Analog*

The Diving Series (Reading Order):

NOVELS

THE RUNABOUT

A DIVING NOVEL

KRISTINE KATHRYN RUSCH

*wmg*PUBLISHING

The Runabout

Published 2017 by WMG Publishing
www.wmgpublishing.com
First published in Asimov's Science Fiction, *May/June 2017*
Cover and layout copyright © 2017 by WMG Publishing
Cover design by Allyson Longueira/WMG Publishing
Cover art copyright © Philcold/Dreamstime
ISBN-13: 978-1-56146-794-5
ISBN-10: 1-56146-794-4

This one is for the fans.
I hope you have as much fun reading this book as I had writing it.

THE RUNABOUT

A DIVING NOVEL

1

CHORAL MUSIC. SIXTEEN VOICES, perfect harmony, singing without words. Chords shifting in a pattern. First, third, fifth, minor sixth, and down again.

I can hear them, running up and down the scales like a waterfall, their chorus twice as loud as the rest of the music floating through the Boneyard.

Of course, I know there is no music here. I am hearing the malfunctioning tech of a thousand, five thousand, ten thousand ships, all clustered together in an area of space larger than some planets. The sound is the way that my head processes the changing energy signatures, although, oddly, I can't hear any of it when I have my exterior communications link off.

Anyone with a genetic marker that ties them to the Fleet can hear this. Everyone else can't.

Although I've never really tested this assumption thoroughly. I don't know if those of us with the marker hear the same thing.

My mind is wandering, which is dangerous during a dive. I have just exited the *Sove*, a Dignity Vessel we pulled from the Boneyard months ago, and I'm heading toward a completely intact Dignity Vessel only a few meters away. I'm wearing an upgraded environmental suit with more features than I've ever used before. I hate those, but I've finally gotten used to the clear hood that seals around the neck instead of a helmet like I used to wear.

We've sent a line from the *Sove's* smallest bay door to the only visible door on the Dignity Vessel, and I'm clinging to that line by my right hand.

I'm facing the Dignity Vessel when the sound catches me.

Elaine Seager, one of the original Six who learned to dive with me way after we discovered the need for markers, is slowly working her way toward the other Dignity Vessel. She's ever so slightly ahead of me on the line. I was the second one to exit the *Sove*.

Orlando Rea, another one of the Six, is waiting to exit the *Sove*. We have strict procedure about the distance between divers on a line.

In fact, we have strict procedures about everything.

The procedures keep us safe.

"What's the holdup?" Yash Zarlengo asks from inside the *Sove*. She's monitoring us. She hates diving, and avoids it as much as possible.

She'll have to do a lot of it on this trip—she often has to dive when we're in the Boneyard—but she's going to dive only after we know what's inside our target vessel.

I snap to attention, still caught by that sound.

"I'm the holdup," I say. "Orlando, you need to go around me and catch up to Elaine."

"Not procedure, Boss," Orlando says from behind me. His tone is half-amused, half-chiding. I'm the one who always harps on procedure.

But he does as I ask. He exits the bay door on the right side instead of the left, and grips the line.

I flip my comm so that Yash can't hear what I have to say to the other two divers.

"You hearing that?" I ask.

Orlando looks around—up, down, sideways. There are ships everywhere. Different kinds, different makes, different eras. As far as we can tell, they're all Fleet vessels, although some of our team back at the Lost Souls Corporation hopes that we'll also find vessels we've never seen before.

There's a theory that these ships were stored here during a protracted war.

I think the theory's wishful thinking. Because I love diving ancient and abandoned ships, I've learned a lot about history. And one thing that unites human beings, no matter where they live, is their ability to take a historical fact and discard it for a story that sounds ever so much better.

The war sounds so much better than a ship graveyard, put here to store abandoned ships until they're needed—a kind of junkyard in space.

I've stopped arguing that point of view, though. I figure time will tell us what this place actually is.

I can't see Orlando's face through his hood. He has turned away from me.

I wish the new suits had one more feature. I wish we could monitor each other's physical reactions in real time. We send that information back to the *Sove* as we dive, but we don't give it to each other.

I didn't help with the design of the new suits, and that was a mistake. Yash designed them to handle the constantly changing energy waves we identified inside the Boneyard. The waves come from all the *anacapa* drives inside the Boneyard and, Yash thinks, from the Boneyard's *anacapa* drives as well. Each drive has a different signature, and malfunctioning drives have even stranger signatures.

We hit the waves as we move across the emptiness from one ship to another, sometimes one wave in the short distance, and sometimes three dozen waves.

Orlando's hand remains tightly wrapped around the line.

"Yeah," he says softly, in answer to my question. "I do hear that. I can't tell where it's coming from."

Elaine has stopped a few meters from us.

"Are we diving or not?" she asks.

That annoyed question went across the open channel, which means Yash heard it.

"Is there a holdup?" she asks again. "Besides Boss?"

I decide to come clean. "We've got a strange energy signature."

"I'm not reading anything from your suits," she says.

3

I sigh silently. We're now getting to the thing she hates—the musicality of the Boneyard itself.

"I can hear it," I say.

"Me, too," Orlando says. He doesn't have to. I hope he's not protecting me.

Even though Yash represents the Fleet on these dives, I'm in charge of them. I still run the Lost Souls Corporation, even if I've delegated many of my duties to Ilona Blake.

I never go on dives where someone else is in charge.

"Well," Yash says, "whatever you 'hear' isn't important. Examining that ship ahead of you is."

She's right. We are salvaging ships from the Boneyard, and it takes a lot of work. We've taken seventeen Dignity Vessels so far, but not all of them work as well as we want them to. We've ended up using six of them for parts.

Orlando turns toward me, remembering, maybe at this late date, that I'm the one who gives the final orders here.

I nod, then sigh.

"She's right," I say. "We're on the clock. Let's keep moving forward."

2

EACH DIVE RUNS ON A TIMETABLE. It's a trick I learned decades ago, when I started wreck diving with teams. If you don't have a timetable, you can't measure your progress.

You also can't measure your failure.

And often, you have no idea something has gone wrong until it's much too late.

It's nearly impossible to maintain a consistent clock in the Boneyard. That's something we've been working on since we started diving it. The *anacapa* waves skew the recording of passing time in various kinds of tech.

My biggest fear is that they'll actually change the way the divers experience time, as opposed to the way that the crew on the *Sove* experiences it.

That differential killed my mother at the abandoned Fleet starbase that we called the Room of Lost Souls. She did not have the genetic marker, and time passed quickly for her. I was with her: time passed the same for me as it did for those outside the room.

Here in the Boneyard, my dive team and I have seen some strange changes due to the *anacapa* waves—mostly in suit measurements to be sure—but I worry that the differential that killed my mother will also kill us.

I've discussed this repeatedly with Yash. We've compensated (we hope) for the differential with the suits. But we're being excessively cautious on every dive in the Boneyard.

We begin our planning back at the Lost Souls Corporation. Which, yes, I named for the Room of Lost Souls, partly as a way to remember that everything we deal with in our work is extremely dangerous.

When we first entered the Boneyard nine months ago now, we scanned the entire yard—we *hope* anyway. (I'm not so sure.) We found more ships than we can dive in our lifetimes, more ships than a thousand of us can dive in our lifetimes.

So, we're trying to cherry-pick what we need, and even that's hard, since we have diverse needs.

Yash, and the crew of the *Ivoire,* who got stranded here, 5,000 years in their future, because of a malfunctioning *anacapa* drive, want to find a way to rejoin the Fleet.

I want enough Dignity Vessels to protect us against the Empire. We've had several skirmishes with them not too long ago. With some savvy Fleet tactics and the element of surprise, we won those skirmishes. But I suspect we won't remain victors forever.

At some point, the Lost Souls Corporation—and the Nine Planets Alliance, which houses us—will gain the attention of the Empire all over again, and we'll need more than the military savvy and surprise to fight them.

We'll need better ships.

The Fleet's Dignity Vessels are those ships.

So, back at Lost Souls, we pick the vessel or vessels we're going to try to pull out of the Boneyard, and then we come here, get as close as we can with the *Sove,* and explore the chosen ship. Twice, we decided the Dignity Vessels we dove were too damaged to take back to Lost Souls. The rest, we dove, and then we reactivated the ships, sending them back to Lost Souls using their own *anacapa* drives.

It's been scary and exhilarating, and something I enjoy more than all the politics and business combined.

We remain organized with our dives when we arrive. As excited as some of us get (as *I* get), we make sure we follow our plan to the letter.

That means the first thing we do, after settling in, is hook the *Sove* and the chosen ship with a grappling line. Then we map the line.

We noticed on our very first dive in the Boneyard all those months ago that the line seems to wobble when it leaves the ship and grips the other ship. As far as we've been able to tell, that wobble isn't an actual bobble, a movement caused by a force exerted on the line.

It's a perception, as the line goes through different *anacapa* waves, and experiences time slightly differently in each wave. We can actually see the changes the line goes through. Those changes register as a wobble, when they are, in reality, a slowing and speeding up, a slight change in course that we can actually see.

That wobble has made us very cautious.

What we do when we map the line is that the dive team—whoever that will be—uses the line to travel outside the *Sove* to the other ship. We have every single piece of data-capture equipment in our suits on. We also have at least one person carrying a small active probe, which records everything.

Then we bring the data back, and we make a map of the changes in *anacapa* waves along the line's path.

The fewest changes we've recorded have been three on a single dive, even though—on that dive—the distance between the ships was the longest we had. The most changes we've recorded has been twenty-five.

So far, we haven't been able to figure out an equation that will help us determine how many changes exist in a particular section of the Boneyard. We estimated that this particular dive will have six different wave changes between us and the new ship, but we don't know that for sure.

That frustrates Yash.

It frustrates me too.

And it worries me. All the unknowns in the Boneyard excite me and terrify me. Whenever I come here, I feel like the young diver I was on my first few wreck dives, when I realized just how little I knew about ancient space ships, and about space itself.

Each dive since those early dives has been a challenge.

Each dive in the Boneyard takes that original challenge and ratchets it up by a factor of one hundred.

We're doing something crazy here.

And for that reason, I'm enjoying myself immensely.

3

Right now, our task is to map the line. We need to know where all the waves are. We also need to know if there are readings we don't understand.

I've learned the hard way to watch out for things like that.

We're also looking at everything around us.

This particular region of the Boneyard has only a few Dignity Vessels. The one we hope to dive seems to date from the same time period as the *Ivoire*, the ship that brought Yash to our time period. The other Dignity Vessels that we've captured have been newer than the *Ivoire*, and while the *Ivoire's* engineering staff likes that, they're also intimidated by it.

They want something familiar, so we decided to come to this part of the Boneyard. Our original scans noted the Dignity Vessels here were older than the ones near the first dives we took months ago.

We weren't able to judge the age of the other nearby ships. These are small vessels, planet hoppers, runabouts, and fighters, things used for short distances. The Fleet also uses them as decoys. That way, the populations of the planets the Fleet approaches have no idea that hundreds of large ships are in the area.

The Fleet also uses its small ships to explore planets and other areas, and also to fight some of its battles.

Or perhaps I should say *used*, since we have no idea if the Fleet still follows that practice, or if the Fleet still even exists.

I keep those thoughts to myself most of the time. The surviving crew of the *Ivoire* chooses to believe that the Fleet still exists, and fights with me when I say it doesn't. I stopped mentioning it—not because I changed my mind, but because the fights are worthless without proof.

I also came to a realization as I indulged in those fights. I was arguing theory. The *Ivoire* crew was talking about their lives. They *needed* to believe the Fleet still existed, more than I needed to convince them that it didn't. They needed something from their past life to hold on to. It kept them moving forward.

I'm moving forward now, slowly, because the music bothers me. It seems to bother Orlando as well, but Elaine hasn't really noticed it. She hates mapping the line, even though it's necessary.

Before we go, we always choose the direction we'll hang from the line. We generally mimic the position of the ship we've embarked from. The ship's artificial gravity creates a sense of up and down that lingers when we do short dives. So we head out in such a way that we can easily get back into the airlock and remain on our feet.

That means our up is the ship's up, and our down is the ship's down. It makes discussions easier later—even when we get to the other ship, which will have no artificial gravity on at all. That ship will be tilted, and maybe the ceiling will be our down, but we don't need to worry about it—not when we're in the mapping phase.

The choral music seems even louder as I progress along the line. My stomach has knotted and I know soon that Mikk, who is monitoring all of our vitals, will give me the usual caution about the gids. The gids mean that my heart rate is elevated, I'm breathing too rapidly, and my adrenaline is up.

That almost always happens to me early in a dive. It's so common for me that those who dive with me usually ignore my first five minutes of data—what would be gids for other divers. But I suspect my heart rate has been elevated longer than usual.

I force myself to breathe evenly, and as I do, I realize what's bothering me.

The music should be thin here. The only *anacapa* drives around us should be from the Dignity Vessel we're going to dive, and the *Sove*. The

Sove's *anacapa* drive is just fine. I'm assuming—we're all assuming—the drive on the Dignity Vessel we're going to explore is malfunctioning.

We should hear that Dignity Vessel's *anacapa* over everything else, a strong kind of reverberating music of some kind or another. And then, faintly, the sounds of other malfunctioning drives much farther away.

But this music is strong. Either there's a very powerful *anacapa* drive breaking down somewhere far from here—so powerful, in fact, that we can hear it (feel it, experience it, *whatever*) from far away—or something else nearby has an *anacapa* drive.

"I'm stopping for a moment," I say to everyone. I need to look around.

"You okay?" This is Mikk from inside the *Sove*. Those vitals, again.

"I'm fine, but something's odd out here. Orlando, Elaine, please look around and see what we're missing. Mikk, are there other Dignity Vessels in the area?"

As I say that last, I wince. The *Ivoire* crew hates the term "Dignity Vessel," but most of us still use it as shorthand when the *Ivoire* crew isn't around.

"The closest is half a kilometer away," Mikk says. "And that's measuring on the diagonal."

What he's telling me is that the sound should be even fainter with that direct measure.

"Thanks," I say.

"What's going on?" Yash asks. "Are you coming back to the ship?"

"No," I say. "We're going to assess something."

I shut off contact with the *Sove* again, and say to both Orlando and Elaine, "See if you see part of a Dignity Vessel nearby. Maybe there's a loose *anacapa*."

They both acknowledge me. Then I hook my comm back to the *Sove*. I keep Yash and Mikk out of the loop because I don't want them to focus on the wrong things. I want those of us diving to figure out what we can from here. Then we'll turn to the map we made of the Boneyard months ago.

That map isn't complete. Nor does it show small bits and pieces of other ships. I don't want to make assumptions about what's around us based on partial data.

So, I'm looking at everything. Above me hover two single-seater fighters of a design that Yash tells me got abandoned years before she started as an engineer (so well over 5,000 years ago). Even with repairs, those fighters will never fly on their own again.

Five planet hoppers cluster below me, and they seem to be in good shape, although I can't really tell from above.

Directly in front of me, of course, is the Dignity Vessel that we're planning to dive, and to my right, a runabout that is pockmarked with age. I've never seen that model before. It looks old.

Pieces of other ships gather around us, but I don't see any loose engineering sections or bits of tech. I see nothing that should have an *anacapa* drive except the Dignity Vessel.

Yash has told me over and over again that *anacapa* drives do not belong in small ships. That's a tenet of the Fleet. That tenet prevents the small ships from accidentally traveling elsewhere too rapidly with no backup.

Anacapa drives enable Fleet vessels to travel through a fold in space. The vessels can actually stop in foldspace, and spend time there, time that is different than time in the part of space they left.

The Fleet has argued throughout its existence about the nature of foldspace and what, exactly, an *anacapa* drive does. It always bothers me that the Fleet relies so heavily on technology it doesn't understand.

Of course, I now rely on it as well.

Ships can travel through entire sectors of space using the *anacapa* drive—ending up almost unimaginable distances from here. The Fleet occasionally uses the *anacapa* drive to get out of a bad situation: a ship in the middle of a firefight will hop into foldspace for an hour or so, and return to the area where the fight had occurred half a day or a week later.

The risk for small ships is that they get out too far from the Fleet, and have no way to return to the Fleet in a timely manner. Most small ship pilots aren't as experienced as the crew that runs the Dignity Vessels, and therefore are prone to making serious mistakes.

Yash also believes that *anacapa* drives are too powerful for small ships. She thinks that *anacapa* drives could damage a smaller ship, although she has yet to explain the science of that to me.

She and I had a heck of an argument almost a year ago now, when I made her put an *anacapa* drive into a skip so that we could dive the Boneyard.

She did as I asked, even though, it turned out, we didn't need that drive to get into the Boneyard. The drive actually kept us out of the Boneyard, since the Boneyard's shield technology actively blocks unfamiliar *anacapa* drives from entering—something my brain has still been assessing ever since we got that piece of information on our first dive here.

"Is that sound coming from the Dignity Vessel?" I ask Elaine and Orlando.

"I don't think so," Elaine says. She's the closest to the Dignity Vessel. "It's fainter here than it was near the *Sove*."

I don't like the sound of that. It means that something we're not seeing might actually be threatening the *Sove*.

I let out a small sigh. This isn't something we can solve from the line. We need to do some more investigative work, and we need to do it quickly.

We don't want to lose the *Sove* in here.

"I'm aborting this mission," I say.

Elaine and Orlando both turn toward me, and I don't have to see their faces through their hoods to know they're registering shock.

I almost never abort dives, and if I do, I don't do it this early. I never do it when there's no obvious threat or no injury.

But something feels off about this entire dive.

They don't question me, though. They immediately turn around, and start pulling themselves back to the *Sove*.

I travel with them, listening to that choral music running up and down a diatonic scale. I know that this isn't music. I know it's something else entirely. But it sounds like voices raised in song.

And, more ominously, I find it beautiful.

4

I LEVER MYSELF THROUGH THE small bay door right after Orlando, feeling a little chilled. We're diving out of this side of the *Sove* instead of one of the main entrances because it's easier. The equipment we need is strapped against the walls to prevent it from floating away.

The environmental systems are off in here, and we've kept the door open to the Boneyard, a risk that Yash believes we can take, since the doors to the interior of the *Sove* are sealed shut.

There's no airlock in the bay because it's designed to launch the kind of small ships that now litter this part of the Boneyard. However, this part of the bay is one of the most solidly built sections of a Dignity Vessel. Dignity Vessels are amazingly well built. But, when we decided to use the *Sove* as our main diving ship, we reinforced it with a layer of brand-new nanobits, strengthening the standard design.

We also reinforced the interior of this bay, for an added layer of protection.

It's probably overkill. The *Sove* is more ship than we need. The Fleet's large-sized ships, the ones people of my era call Dignity Vessels, but the Fleet just calls "ships," are built for five hundred to a thousand people. Most of those people are not crew. A single Dignity Vessel can be a small city, with doctors and psychiatrists and chefs and artists and teachers as well as engineers and military personnel. Or the Dignity Vessel has a particular purpose, like some of the school ships that the captain of the *Ivoire*, Jonathan "Coop" Cooper, has told me about.

Most of the people on a DV don't touch the equipment that make the ship run. As a result, the ship can run well with a skeleton crew of less than twenty. But it can also function with a crew of four, if need be.

I've only flown on a Dignity Vessel with a full complement of crew a few times, back in the early days of the *Ivoire*'s arrival in this time period. Since then, many people in the *Ivoire*'s crew have gone on to other lives or different careers. It's been years since the *Ivoire* was fully staffed.

Now, at Lost Souls, we're training new Dignity Vessel crew members, because we have other Dignity Vessels. We never fully staff the ships. We don't have enough people yet.

On this trip, we have a crew of forty, many of them divers, which means that the *Sove* is much more ship than we need.

However, Yash argued for Dignity Vessels to dive the Boneyard. After our second trip here, I finally saw the wisdom in her argument.

She likes the power of a Dignity Vessel—the weaponry, the ability to jump into foldspace and get away quickly—combined with the space of the bays. In the future, she wants us to fill the *Sove*'s six cargo bays with small ships, so that we won't just have Dignity Vessels at Lost Souls, we will have all the backup ships as well.

Her plans are all wise. I'm happier in the larger vessel, even though I hadn't thought I would be.

And I love the idea of taking the smaller ships back to Lost Souls. We can revive some of the ships, and cobble the others for parts. Best of all, we can learn from their tech.

Diving with a purpose other than exploration. Salvage, in a way that I never thought I would do.

I also like having the Dignity Vessel at my disposal, especially here in the Boneyard. Since our run-ins with the Empire, we've been using Dignity Vessels to patrol the border between the Nine Planets Alliance and the Empire. The Nine Planets have been using other ships as well, but none of those ships compare to a Dignity Vessel.

I had initially thought we would use all but two of our Dignity Vessels to patrol that border. I figured that, as we got more and more Dignity Vessels, our patrols would increase.

But I lack a military mind. I also had no idea what it took to fly these things.

Both Yash and Coop convinced me to use the *Sove* as a training ship. Twenty of our forty-member crew are in training, learning how to run all of the equipment on board in an actual mission, rather than in some kind of simulation.

In addition to Yash, who focuses on the mission itself, there's always someone from the *Ivoire*'s original crew on the *Sove*, running the trainees. This time, we're focusing mostly on engineering, so Zaria Diaz is in charge of them on this trip. Zaria was second engineer when the *Ivoire* arrived in our timeline.

I have no idea what Zaria's rank is now. Coop's been trying to keep up with the Fleet protocols, which I find rather ridiculous. But I don't tell him that either.

Elaine enters the bay doors last. She pushes away from the doors. I retract the line, then close the doors. They close slowly, a design feature that I usually appreciate, but I dislike greatly in this circumstance.

The sound of the Boneyard haunts me until the doors finally press closed. I let out a small sigh, as if I've been under pressure myself, then I reach over to the wall, and reestablish environmental controls.

As the artificial gravity slowly reasserts itself, we float to the bay's floor. We wait until our suits register a full environment before pulling off our hoods.

The bay's normal internal silence feels like an emptiness, and that thought horrifies me as well. Not just on a conscious level, but on a subconscious one: the hair on the back of my neck is literally standing on end.

I resist the urge to swipe at it. It'll settle down when I do.

I wonder if Mikk is still monitoring my vitals. I wonder how they read when I'm deeply horrified.

"What's wrong?" Orlando asks.

I'm not sure I can explain it all to him. I'm not even going to try, at least not in here.

"Let's meet with Yash and the other divers," I say, as a deliberate dodge.

The time it'll take to assemble everyone will give me a few moments to myself.

It'll give me a moment to shake off my past.

5

MY MOTHER'S FINAL WORDS were *Beautiful. Oh, so beautiful.*

I know this, because I was the only one who heard them.

My mother and I got trapped inside part of the Room of Lost Souls. She died horribly in there, aging at a rapid rate. By the time my father pulled her out, she was little more than a skeleton.

I was fine. Terrified, but fine.

I have the genetic marker that protects someone exposed to malfunctioning *anacapa* drives. My mother did not.

And the Room of Lost Souls wasn't really a room. It was a large starbase built thousands of years ago by the Fleet. Coop had visited it many times when it was active. Then, it was known as Starbase Kappa. In his memory, it was a living, breathing space station. Once he arrived here, he heard what it had become.

He had actually led a mission there to deactivate the malfunctioning *anacapa* in the station, so that more people would not die.

The station's malfunctioning drive shut down too late for my mother and hundreds, maybe thousands, of others.

But after I learned about *anacapa* drives and the way that the genetic marker interacted with them, I thought the temptations at the Room of Lost Souls only beckoned the unwary.

Today, on this dive, was the first time I've had to reassess that assumption. I've loved the Boneyard since my first dive here—a passionate, rather unreasonable, love.

But I always assumed that love was based in my own history. I am a historian. I love old things. I love wrecks, and I love mysteries—ancient mysteries—wrapped in technology.

The Boneyard is almost tailor-made for me.

Today, though…today, I felt something different. I felt an attraction to something so strong that I could have lost myself in it. I could have walked into that sound forever, the way that my mother's hands reached for the lights she saw that accompanied the sounds she heard.

I'm still not sure if she was aware of the fact she'd been dying that day—those days (at least for her). I'm not sure if she would have changed anything *had* she been aware of it.

She had been completely captivated by the energy around her.

As I was today.

And that's why I aborted the mission.

I was scared, for the first time in a long time.

I don't admit that to the others, though. If I do, they'll never let me dive the Boneyard again. Even though I'm the one in charge of everything, I can't dive alone, and they know that. No one will accompany me. Everyone will consider me dangerous.

And I find myself wondering: Am I dangerous?

I let the thought slide off me as I head to the conference room. We've commandeered the nicest conference room near the bridge. One of the culinary staff keeps it constantly supplied with fresh coffee, tea, and water, as well as each diver's favorite personal beverage. There's fresh fruit as well, and some pastries for those of us who like to indulge.

The food doesn't look good to me at the moment. I'm still too wrapped up in the dive.

Instead, my gaze goes to the holographic map of the Boneyard that we've managed to assemble over the months. The Boneyard is huge, and it has blank spots that we can't seem to map no matter what kind of equipment we use. We're probably going to have to explore it with a Dignity Vessel, but I'm not ready to do that yet. And neither is anyone else.

My gaze goes to the holographic map, and then to the smaller representation of the area we have chosen to dive. Our target ship is a different color than the other ships in that model, just so that we know exactly what we're looking at.

Someone has updated that map to include the *Sove* as well.

I'm the last to arrive, which surprises me. I only stopped in my cabin for a minute to change out of the clothes I wear underneath my suit. I didn't even take time to shower. I splashed cool water on my face, and then came directly here.

Mikk sits at the head of the table. He's been at my side for years. He's one of the best divers I've ever known, and he rarely complains about not being able to dive things like the Boneyard. We can't send him unprotected into the Boneyard, but Fleet-designed ships protect people without the genetic marker from a malfunctioning *anacapa* drive.

Yash and Coop had told me that for a long time before I was willing to test it. And, if I was being honest with myself, I had been unwilling to test it at all. Mikk and a few other members of Lost Souls had decided to test it themselves.

They had known they could die, and they hadn't cared.

I like that kind of courage in the face of exploration, and I hate it at the same time. Especially when people I care about test things that scare me.

And malfunctioning *anacapa* drives scare me.

Of course, Yash was right. She knew Fleet tech better than any of us.

However, she can't convince me to let Mikk (or any of the others without the genetic marker) dive the Boneyard.

I don't want to risk his life based on the strength of the suit technology. We know the layers of nanobit construction protect him in the *Sove*, but the environmental suits are simply one thin layer against a cold and unforgiving universe.

Mikk himself has never argued to go on these Boneyard dives.

Right now, he watches me, arms folded in front of himself, and there's something in his eyes, an unease, maybe? He looks as strong as ever, but his face is set in a hard line.

Yash sits next to him. She looks as strong as he does. Like Mikk, she was raised in real gravity, and it shows in the thickness of her bones and the layers of muscle along her powerful body. She wears her hair short so that she doesn't have to deal with it, although at the moment, it could use a comb.

So could Orlando's. He doesn't look like he's done anything except remove his suit. He looks tiny compared to the two of them—a true wreck diver, the kind of thin, wiry man who can go into every nook and cranny.

He didn't start diving until I found him, thanks to an Empire study of people who could survive in what they called "stealth tech." Stealth tech was really *anacapa* waves, but the Empire didn't know that.

I'm not sure they know it now.

And Elaine sits at the foot of the table, chewing on the cuticle on her left thumb. That surprises me. Elaine, who is nearest to my age, is usually calm. That's one of the reasons I like diving with her. She's generally unflappable.

I grab some water, then sit down. I'm still a little emotionally unsettled. That callback to my mother's death upset me more than I want to consider.

Yash frowns at me. "You aborted the mission without discussing it with me," she said.

She doesn't dive—or rather, doesn't dive much. She's used to a more military structure. Even if we were operating in a military structure right now—and we aren't—I'm in charge of the dives.

But I'm not going to fight with her about that. Not here, not in front of the others.

Maybe not ever.

Because, on one level, she's right: we should discuss before aborting early in a dive, especially given the time and resources we spend getting here.

"That's right," I say after I take a sip of the water. "We couldn't stay out there."

"We saw no danger there," she say.

"I know," I say, "and that might be a problem."

She frowns at me. So does Mikk. But Elaine is nodding, and Orlando looks as unsettled as I feel.

"What happened?" Yash asks.

"There's another malfunctioning *anacapa* drive," I say, "and we couldn't spot it from the line."

I explain the music without going into detail about how beautiful it is. How it lured me. I do mention how loud it was, and Elaine adds that she couldn't hear it as strongly close to the ruined Dignity Vessel we had targeted.

Yash's frown grows deeper. She looks at Orlando, as if asking him for confirmation of what we're saying.

"The sound was strong," he says. "And I didn't see any ship it could have come from."

We all turn, almost as a unit, to that area holomap of the Boneyard. I scan it, looking for any kind of Dignity Vessel that would be close enough to cause the reaction the three of us had.

We had deliberately chosen this particular Dignity Vessel because it was close to our entry point into the Boneyard, it was located near the edge of the Boneyard, and there weren't other Dignity Vessels around it. We are still a bit skittish, worried that maybe we are being watched.

The Boneyard itself had fired on us once, as we were taking ships out of it the very first time. We don't know if the Boneyard can attack us while we're inside the Boneyard. We also don't know if the Boneyard will attack us using its shielding equipment, or if some of these ships are set up to act as security around the Boneyard, when something triggers a built-in automated response.

I like to think that no one would have designated a ship with a malfunctioning *anacapa* to defend the Boneyard, but we still don't know, exactly, what this place is, so we're not sure what we're facing.

Yash leans toward the area holomap, peering at it as if it provides answers. She's slowly shaking her head.

"None of the small ships should have *anacapa* drives," she says, "and you didn't see bits of equipment floating loosely."

"We didn't," I confirm, even though she really wasn't asking me. She was just reiterating what I had said, as if she was trying to process it all.

"Hmm," she says. "There's no real empty area around here, where something could be shielded. Unless…"

"Unless?" I ask.

She shakes her head firmly, as if dismissing the idea.

"Unless?" I press.

She looks over at me. "Unless they've masked a signature. What we're reading as a group of small ships isn't."

"Can they do that?" I ask.

Anger flashes in her eyes, but it disappears almost as quickly as it appears. Then she shrugs as if she's calm, which she clearly is not.

"I have no idea what the Fleet can or cannot do," she says. "Five thousand years ago, no, we couldn't do that. And we haven't discovered that technology in any of the ships we've pulled so far."

"Then," I say slowly, "why are you mentioning it as a possibility?"

"Because," she says. "Everything is a possibility now. I have the feeling that if we can imagine it, it might have already been built."

Sounds magical to me, but I'm not going to say that. I know the weight of time has fallen on the crew of the *Ivoire* in a way that I don't entirely understand.

I also know that we can't be chasing phantoms, when we're faced with real challenges.

I need to learn that as well. My mother is phantom. What happened to her happened decades ago, and I am a different person, in a different place.

"We don't have the technology either," I say. "Not Lost Souls, not the Nine Planets, not the Empire. So let's go with what we know."

Yash doesn't move for a moment, and I wonder if she even heard me. Then she slaps a hand on the table. It vibrates, but the holomap doesn't. It looks constant and unchanging.

"You did the right thing, aborting," she says.

I don't want to acknowledge that. Of course, I did the right thing. And I don't have to justify it. Not even now.

"We need to scan. We need to investigate every little corner of this part of the Boneyard. We can't send anyone out there again until we know."

She looks at me as if she expects me to back her up. I smile just a little, because I can't help it.

Yes, we need to do those things. Yes, I already had that thought. Yes, that's why I aborted the mission.

But I don't say that. I don't need to.

She looks surprised at my expression, and then she smiles, just a little sheepishly. She doesn't apologize—Yash rarely apologizes—but she shrugs again.

"It'll take some time," she says.

"I know," I say, and realize I'm calmer than I've been since we get back.

Now we're in familiar territory for me. Dive a little, research a lot, look for hazards, account for the hazards, dive again.

Mikk leans back, out of Yash's range of vision, and gives me a small grin. He approves.

He also knows, as I do, that we have a lot of work to do before we can dive again.

6

AFTER OUR MEETING, Yash disappears into Engineering. She is going to work with all the trainees and Zaria. They're going to design a program to account for the masking that Yash is talking about. It has to do with spatial relations and size, and maybe something existing half-in and half-out of foldspace.

I think that's all too complicated. So does Mikk. He and I sit in the conference room long after Yash has left.

I grab a slice of bread, spread some whitish-purple sauce on it that tastes vaguely of plums, and top it with shredded carrots. Then I fold it in half. A makeshift meal until I can get a real one.

I set the meal next to my water, and sit back down. Mikk hasn't moved.

"So what's really bothering you?" he asks.

I'm not sure if he's asking that because of the readings on my suit from earlier or because he knows me well enough to know there's more to the story than what I told Yash.

Or both.

"We need to check those small ships," I say.

"Yash says the Fleet doesn't put *anacapa* drives in small ships," Mikk says.

"I know what Yash says." I take a bite out of the sandwich. It's better than I expected. Or I'm hungrier than I thought I was. "I also know her information on the Fleet is five thousand years old."

He stares at me for a moment, probably shocked that I said that aloud. We've all been very circumspect in how we deal with the *Ivoire* crew. They're fragile people, even though they've been in our timeline for years now.

We don't discuss how long they've been here, how old their information is, how wrong they might be. We try to be kind to them, because we're in an odd circumstance.

Even though their tech is 5,000 years old, it's more advanced than ours. A few of the staff at Lost Souls, particularly César Voris, a historian who has worked with me for years, believe that it's possible the modern Fleet—if there is such a thing—are as backwards as we are now.

Over centuries, we lost our tech. Lots of knowledge has completely disappeared. It's possible that the same thing happened to the Fleet.

Of course, if I bank on that, then I'm making the same mistakes that Yash is. I'm basing my opinions of the way the universe works on the way that the universe works in *my* time period, not in all others.

"You think the Fleet added *anacapa* drives to small ships?" Mikk sounds incredulous. "You think they actually got past all of those fears that Yash brings up every time we mention adding *anacapa* drives to our skips?"

"She got past it once," I say. "We have a skip with an *anacapa*."

"And she blames you for it," he says.

"As she should," I say. "It was my idea. And it's my responsibility if anything goes wrong."

Mikk leans back, tilting his chair just enough so that he can reach the sideboard without getting up. He grabs a spotted apple, one of his favorite things.

He doesn't eat it, though. He clutches it as if it's a ball and he's about to throw it.

"We have enough staff on this ship," he says after a moment. "We can actually run the scans without disturbing the calculations she's doing."

"You and I can run the scans," I say. "It's not hard. It's probably not even going to be time-consuming."

He grins at me. "You're going rogue, Boss."

I give him a sideways, disapproving look, even though I'm amused at his tone.

"Why is that funny?" I ask.

"Because you own the company," he says. "You don't have to hide from your employees."

I've been hiding from my employees ever since I got employees. Especially employees whose names I can't remember, if I learned them at all. Lost Souls now employs more people than some starbases.

"Technically," I say, becoming serious, "Yash isn't one of my employees."

"Yeah," he says, "but everyone else is."

I know, and there are days—weeks, months, even—when that bothers me. I like to pretend, as I'm doing right now, like I'm back in my own ship, *Nobody's Business*, and I'm dealing with a small crew hired for one particular job.

I hired Mikk for several jobs in the past, before he became an employee of Lost Souls. In some ways, going rogue with him, as he said, will feel like old times.

I smile.

"Let's do this thing," I say.

He smiles in return. "Thought you'd never ask."

7

MIKK AND I GO TO MY SUITE. I have commandeered the captain's suite. When we first started using the *Sove*, I hadn't wanted a suite that big. It's a small apartment with two bedrooms, a living area, a full kitchen, a large bathroom, and an entire other small apartment's worth of equipment.

It was the equipment that ultimately convinced me to make the suite mine. Because buried in the specs for that suite, as Coop showed me one afternoon, is a backup bridge.

If I have to, I can fly this entire ship by myself from the suite.

Not that I can comfortably fly a Dignity Vessel. But I've learned enough to get us home in an emergency.

And this little room, with its backup bridge, makes the captain's suite too dangerous to give to someone else or even leave unattended. So I took it, and hope I never have to use it.

The backup bridge is built for one person to use comfortably, but two can squeeze into it. There's a pilot's chair, lots of navigational equipment, a space for holoimages, and a large screen on the far wall.

There's also more computing power than I have ever had on any ship I ever used for diving.

It's that computing power that I want right now.

Mikk and I squeeze into the backup bridge. I sit in the pilot's chair. He stands behind me, uncomfortably close. I can see his reflection on the navigational board.

I am not sure how much he knows about the backup bridge. He knows it's here, but I'm not sure he knows how to use it.

I should probably teach him, since in some ways, I trust him more than I trust Yash.

I lean so that Mikk can see over my shoulder, and hit the very first commands Coop ever taught me.

I isolate the backup bridge from the regular bridge and from engineering. No one in those departments will know that I'm using the equipment here.

I'm not sure why I'm being so secretive. If someone were to ask me, I'd say it's because being secretive is a habit for me. I've always kept my own counsel.

But there's more to it than that. A couple impulses, in fact.

I don't want Yash to know that I think she's chasing fantasies. I'm being protective of yet another *Ivoire* crew member.

I also don't want an argument from her. I want to present a *fait accompli* if, indeed, I do find something.

I tap one more control on the board. A rather uncomfortable stool-like chair rises out of the floor near the other side of the room.

"That's yours, I'm afraid," I say to Mikk.

He grins, then heads over and sits down. I transfer his identification data to the other board, and he runs through his own personal ID sequence.

Then we begin.

Mikk and I have done this kind of search before, long before Lost Souls became as big as it is. We have old programs that look for malfunctioning "stealth tech," which is what we thought *anacapa* drives were, before we learned about the Fleet.

Those scans work better than some of the Fleet-designed scans because ours are built to look for *malfunctioning* tech, not *anacapa* signatures in general. Plus, ours have been refined over the years to look for very slight signals, where none of the Fleet-designed scans were initially designed to find anything that was near the end of its natural life.

The biggest challenge for Mikk and me isn't finding the malfunctioning *anacapa* signals. It's finding the correct one in a morass of signals.

We will have to examine all of the scans pretty closely, because we don't have time to redesign the program. We need to find whatever this is relatively quickly, in case we're being threatened by something we don't quite comprehend.

We dig in, just like we used to do before we ever met the crew of the *Ivoire*. Before Lost Souls. Before we were anything but a small wreck-diving team with a focus on history, a team that stumbled onto something big, something that changed our small corner of the universe—forever.

Five hours in, we find it. The malfunctioning *anacapa* is in the ancient, damaged runabout I had noticed when we were mapping the line. That runabout had looked like nothing consequential, and yet it's giving off a malfunctioning *anacapa* signal that's stronger than anything I've ever seen.

We leave my quarters, and I take the news to Yash myself.

8

YASH IS WORKING IN THE engineering section of the *Sove*, five levels down from the captain's quarters. It's strange to walk through the nearly empty ship. I've been in a lot of empty Dignity Vessels, now that we have a number of them at Lost Souls, but never while they're in flight.

There's a hum to the ship, a quiet vibration that happens whenever a Dignity Vessel's full life-support system kicks on. The lights, artificial gravity, and temperature controls make some kind of sound that I can sense. Maybe it's similar to the sounds I hear when I'm around malfunctioning *anacapa* drives, because Yash denies that there's any difference between a functioning Dignity Vessel and one that's mostly shut down.

I think she's so used to being on Dignity Vessels that there are sounds and feelings she has tuned out since childhood, things that sound unusual to me.

The humming semi-silence on the *Sove* doesn't unnerve me as much as it makes me uncomfortable. That sense that we're on a ship too large for our mission hits me again.

I make my way to engineering, taking an extra check of my mood. I have calmed down now that we've done the search. I'm far enough away from that music that it seems like I overreacted.

Maybe I did. But I am going to keep an eye on myself.

And before my next dive, I will probably talk to Mikk about that reaction—if I can figure out how to discuss it without getting me sidelined.

31

The engineering section of the *Sove* is really three levels of the ship. Equipment, programs, experimental areas, and teaching areas all exist within the *Sove*, just like most of the Dignity Vessels I've been in.

But Yash and her team are working out of the main engineering area. Doors swish open as I walk into that part of the ship. The front section, buried deep inside the ship itself so that it would be hard to damage, has a strange, pale blue and gold light when it's in use.

I don't understand any of the equipment down here, even though different people have explained it to me in different ways. I know enough about ships to repair my own skip, to use my own single-ship, and to save my own life with modern tech built by the Empire or some private company from my time.

But there's a lot to Fleet-built equipment that makes no sense to me at all—and that's before we get to the *anacapa* drive. The *anacapa* drive, which unnerves me most of all, because no Fleet engineer understands it entirely.

I'm not even sure of the history of the drive, only that it's deeply tied to the Fleet's identity and history. Once the Fleet got *anacapa* drives, it traveled farther than it had before. The *anacapa* drive made the Fleet of old into the Fleet that raised Yash and Coop. The starbases scattered all over sectors, the sector bases built across distances that make my brain hurt, and the Fleet itself, moving ever forward, came about because the *anacapa* drive can take the ships into foldspace for brief moments of time, and then bring them back elsewhere.

The *anacapa* drives also malfunction more than any other part of the ship, which I find nearly unacceptable.

Coop and Yash consider it a fact of life.

Yash is standing in the center of the room, looking at a holomap of the area around the *Sove*. A square box moves through the three-dimensional map, changing color as it goes.

I'm guess that this is the program she designed to see if some Dignity Vessel is masking itself as a smaller vessel.

"Finding anything?" I ask.

She jumps. She clearly did not hear me enter the engineering area.

I don't see the rest of her team, but that means nothing. There are rooms and more rooms off this main area. One floor down is the *anacapa* drive itself, housed in a protective area, even though the drive is relatively small.

That's a change that we've made, something I ordered once we started using Dignity Vessels for patrol and to come back to the Boneyard. The first Dignity Vessel I ever dove had its *anacapa* drive just off the bridge. That ship was older than the *Ivoire*, but the *Ivoire*'s design isn't too much different than that.

Since I've seen a lot of death in malfunctioning *anacapa* fields, I don't like the idea of having an *anacapa* drive so close to critical personnel. If someone dies near an *anacapa* drive, they'll do so because they ventured near the drive, not because the drive is badly placed.

Yash looks at me, blinks as if she isn't quite sure why I'm here, and then straightens. She had been slightly bent as she worked in that model, and apparently, she'd been standing that way for a long time. She puts her hand on her back and stretches just a little. I can hear the muscles pop, something that only happens with those who were land-born, like us.

"I haven't found anything yet," she says, "and I'm thinking that's a good thing. I don't want to find a hidden vessel."

I nod, agreeing.

"This is the third scan we've done," she says. "The first looked for active *anacapa*s in the large ships nearby. We also looked for something that might be designed to keep the Boneyard protected, some special tech that we haven't seen before."

"Good thinking," I say. "I hadn't thought of that."

She lets out a breath, then shakes her arms and wrists. She must have been studying that model for much longer than she realized.

"I'm worried that the Boneyard has a lot of surprises for us," she says. "I'm just not sure how to find them."

Me either, but I don't want to discuss that at the moment. It seems like a tangent.

"Our second scan was to look for a large enough space to fit one of our major ships," she says. "But we didn't find that either. Zaria designed the scan I'm looking at now. We ran it once and found nothing. I'm running it again, slower this time, because you know how new programs are. They often miss things just because of the newness of their designs."

"I know." I don't add that's why I used our older program. I'm not going to rub it in. She can figure that out if she wants, later, after we're done with this trip.

"I'll contact you when we figure out where the signature is coming from," she says. "There's a lot of interference—"

"We found the malfunctioning drive," I say, gently. "Mikk and I."

Yash stops, and blinks hard again, processing. I understand how that feels. I've been so deep in research and work that it takes a while for my brain to switch to something new.

I've just never seen Yash like this. But I've never seen Yash hard at work before either.

"You and Mikk?" she asks.

"Yeah," I say, not explaining further. "The bad *anacapa* signature is coming from the ancient runabout."

I step past her and touch the holographic image of the runabout. It's almost impossible to see at this magnification. Yash is looking at a section of the Boneyard, and the most visible ships are the Dignity Vessels. The runabout looks like an old-fashioned rivet, the kind I found in that very first Dignity Vessel I dove, years and years ago.

Yash shakes her head. "It can't be."

"That's what we thought." I lie to her. I want her to think I believe, as she does, that the Fleet would never use *anacapa* drives in small ships. But I see this as one more piece of evidence that the Fleet she knew is long gone.

"It makes no sense to put an *anacapa* in a vehicle that small," she says, not arguing with me, but instead, arguing with the engineers who designed the thing. Long-dead engineers most likely.

"We have no idea what the Fleet ran up against," I say. "Maybe there was a reason for the change."

"I can't imagine what it would be." Yash moves to a console that I hadn't even noticed. It juts out from the wall not far from us. She taps the surface.

I walk over to her side, skirting the gigantic holomodel.

"It *is* one of our ships," she says more to herself than me. "Or, at least, it uses technology that we designed. The interior design is different than anything I've seen, but that doesn't mean much. If someone added an *anacapa* drive to a runabout, the design would have to change to compensate."

She shakes her head.

"But *anacapa*s are for long distance travel, and runabouts aren't. They can't even hold enough supplies or crew to handle distance travel. At most, a few years of supplies could be stored in the runabout and that's for a small crew, maybe four at most."

Yash looks up at me, a frown furrowing her forehead.

"This makes no sense," she says.

"I know," I say. I agree with that much. I believe her argument against *anacapa* drives in small ships. I'm reluctant to use the skip she modified now, because it has an *anacapa* drive.

Too many things can go wrong.

"The ship is old, too," she adds, more to herself than me. "The nanobits are sloughing off the exterior. That takes centuries to occur."

"Even if there's a malfunctioning *anacapa* field?" I ask.

Yash makes a small curious noise, as if she hadn't thought of that. Her fingers are still moving across the console, searching for something.

She finally lets out a sigh and stops.

"You're right," she says. "There's a slight *anacapa* field here. And I didn't think to look for it. Yet you and Mikk did."

"It's our training," I say, not wanting her to think she's losing her edge. "We look for damaged ships to dive, not at how to improve things that already exist."

Even though she doesn't lift her head from that console, I can see her cheeks move as she smiles.

"You know, Boss," she says, "you present yourself as one tough woman with a hard interior. But you're quite nice when you want to be. You didn't have to smooth things over for me."

I'm a little offended. I don't like being called nice. Nice, to me, means that I'm failing somehow.

"Just being honest," I say, and I am. Mikk and I have different training from Yash.

Then I realize she called me "Boss." She and Coop do their best to avoid the name everyone else uses for me. They don't like the idea of someone else having that moniker, even though I'm not—and never really will be—their boss.

Yash taps something on the console, then straightens. The console's screen goes dark.

I have no idea what she had just done.

She turns toward me.

"If we're going to dive the ship we came for," she says, "we need to deal with this runabout first. That *anacapa* drive on it seems to be in its final death throes."

Was that why its music seemed so alluring to me? Or was there another reason?

"You're seeing that as a problem," I say. "I'm not entirely sure I understand what the problem is."

"I don't know when that *anacapa* was built," she says. "I don't know what it's made out of. I'm not even sure how one can fit inside a runabout comfortably. There might be modifications we don't know about."

"There probably are," I say.

She nods, once, as if she's conceding a point. And maybe she is.

"Yeah," she says, "there probably are. And that's not good."

"Because…?"

"Because dying *anacapa*s can be dangerous and unpredictable. Some blow up. Some activate a field in a large area around the *anacapa* drive itself, sending everything in that area into foldspace. That's the theory, anyway. I've never been near a dying *anacapa*, not this kind, anyway."

I've been around several. And they terrify me.

"And," she adds, "then there's just the possibility that the dying *anacapa* might interact with nearby *anacapa*s."

"And do what?" I ask.

She shrugs. "Take us all somewhere, maybe. Cause a feedback loop of some kind, maybe. Create something that might interfere with the Boneyard itself, maybe."

I grow cold. "If it interacts with the Boneyard," I say slowly, "the Boneyard might attack us again."

"Yeah." She wipes a hand over her mouth, as if she can prevent herself from talking. She doesn't, though. She says, "And then there's the issue of leaving."

"The issue of leaving," I repeat. That sounds ominous. "What exactly are you afraid of?"

Even though I think I know. I want her to say it. She's the *anacapa* expert, not me.

She squares her shoulders and takes a deep breath.

"I'm not sure what will happen when we activate our *anacapa*," she says. "And if we activate ours at the same time as we activate the one on the other ship—"

The Dignity Vessel we plan to dive. We used that same plan months ago, when we needed to get a Dignity Vessel out of the Boneyard quickly.

"—those *anacapa* fields might do something to that runabout's *anacapa* drive, something I can't predict."

I swallow hard. I've heard that activating *anacapa*s—large ones— occasionally creates blowback, which is why Coop always insists on activating a Dignity Vessel's *anacapa* drive away from anything connected to Lost Souls. He says *anacapa*s should be activated as far from anything important as possible, unless it's an emergency.

But I've never heard him or anyone else connected with the Fleet say that the arrival of a ship out of foldspace can cause a problem.

Logically, though, it should.

"Why didn't our *anacapa* drive interact with that runabout's *anacapa* drive when we arrived?" I ask.

She bites her lower lip. She's clearly thinking about this hard.

"My initial response," she says, "is that the *Sove* didn't cause any problems because the largest surge in *anacapa* energy occurs when we activate the drive, not when we shut it off."

"But?" I ask, hearing that word in her tone.

"But there is a change in the nearby energy readings whenever a ship arrives out of foldspace," she says.

I remember. I had been in an underground chamber—the ruins of a Fleet sector base—when the *Ivoire* first arrived, finally freed from its foldspace prison where it had been trapped—ship time—for weeks. In my universe, the real universe, *our* universe, the *Ivoire* had been missing for 5,000 years.

When the *Ivoire* arrived, we registered energy readings. The *Ivoire* also brought the coldness of space with it, and a host of other smaller things, including some condensation. We didn't know it all at the time. We were too startled by a huge ship appearing out of nowhere.

I didn't think about that as we brought the *Sove* back into the Boneyard. Our very presence here has probably made some kind of difference in the nature of the Boneyard itself.

"Be clear," I say, "because I am not the expert. What do you mean, exactly?"

"I don't know," she says. "I really don't. This is all new to me."

We stare at each other.

"Could the reason that *anacapa* is malfunctioning be our fault?" I ask, partly because I will keep turning that particular possibility over and over in my mind if I don't.

"No," she says. "The malfunction isn't our fault. But the acceleration of the deterioration might be. The fact that it's nearly done—or even the power of the energy signal, yeah, that could all be our fault. Just for arriving here."

I curse and rub my hand over the back of my neck. That sends a shiver through me.

"Or," she says, sensing my change in mood, "maybe nothing's different. Maybe there will be no interaction at all. As I said, I have no way to know any of it."

"And no way to model the possibilities?" I ask.

"If we have a lot of time, sure," she says. "But I would think we want to get out of here as fast as possible."

I'm shaking my head before I say anything.

She glances at the holographic map, as if it reinforces her thinking. She's going to argue—*hard*—that we need to return to Lost Souls.

"No, we want that ship." I caught myself before I said Dignity Vessel. "We need to explore it. And we're going to run into all kinds of other issues in the Boneyard when we bring the *Sove* back, even if we go to another section."

I sigh, thinking. Then I walk around the model, looking at the ships of all sizes, scattered haphazardly in the Boneyard itself. The Boneyard holds them in position using yet another kind of technology that we only hazily understand. There's not gravity here, but it's not pure space either. The ships aren't drifting. They've gathered, and they're in a kind of protective bubble.

We're always cautious around *anacapa* drives. We're also cautious with the Boneyard, since there's much we still don't understand.

We've always assumed that the Dignity Vessels have *anacapa* drives. However, we've never approached the other ships as if they have *anacapas*.

This runabout changes everything. We now have to search all the small ships, and make sure that they don't have a functioning drive inside.

"We've done some of the work," I say, more to myself than to her. "We know that the other small ships nearby do not have *anacapa* drives—or if they do, the drives are not functioning at all."

"You know that?" she asks. "Your program is that accurate?"

I give her a small smile.

"We used to search for stealth tech, back before we knew you. It was valuable and it was dangerous. After a bad experience with an early Fleet vessel—" I nearly said "Dignity Vessel" again. "—we tried to stay clear of stealth tech. Which meant we had to search for it all the time."

I didn't tell her about the history with my father, about the Room of Lost Souls, about all the other encounters. I had told Coop, and if he had chosen not to enlighten her or the rest of his crew, that was between them.

"Our program is fairly sophisticated," I say, even though as I utter the words, I wonder if she would think so. Everything we do is primitive by Fleet standards. "We can be pretty certain about the small ships nearby. But outside of this area?" I make a circle with my right forefinger, indicating the area we're in at the moment on the holomap. "We can't be certain at all."

Yash bites her lower lip again, studying the map. She's extremely smart. She knows what I'm saying.

If we abort this entire mission now, then we have to abort missions in the future. We can't come back here if we're afraid of malfunctioning *anacapa* drives.

Although, if we come back, I might suggest we don't bring as many people. It's much more dangerous in here than I had initially thought.

"What do you suggest?" she asks.

"We can shut off that runabout's *anacapa* drive, right?" I ask.

"Maybe," she says. "As I mentioned, I have no idea what they put in that runabout. If the *anacapa* is different from what I'm used to—"

"I won't hold you to it," I say. "I'm just asking if, in theory, we can shut it down, right?"

"Yes," she says. "We can shut it down."

"Because that's what I'd like to do," I say. "I'd like to dive that runabout, get what information we can from it, and shut off the *anacapa* drive."

"I don't think we have time to get all the information we need out of the runabout," she says.

I plan these major diving missions with no end date. You never know what you're going to run into. So the dives take as long as the dives take.

I stand up straighter than I had, turning toward her slightly. "Are we on a clock that I don't know about?"

"I figured we have a couple of weeks," she says, either ignoring my annoyed tone or unconcerned over it. "And if we add the runabout, then we don't have enough time for the other ship."

Clocks and schedules and military precision. This is why I don't like working with the *Ivoire* crew. They want to know everything we're going to do, down to the second.

Dives have to be flexible. Dives cannot be planned.

And it doesn't matter how many times I explain that to people like Yash, they don't understand it.

Rather than have that argument yet again, I simply say, "We'll have time."

She half shakes her head before she catches herself. "You don't think it'll take long to dive the runabout?"

"It's not very big," I say. "We need to map it. Then we have to decide what we're going to do with it."

"Meaning?" she asks.

"Do we just shut down the drive and let it stay here? Or do we take it back to Lost Souls and study it? Or do we do something else entirely?"

She threads her fingers together. I've never seen Yash this nervous. Her nervousness is coming out in small ways.

I'm not entirely sure what she's afraid of.

"And if we can't shut the drive down?" she asks quietly.

There it is, the thing that frightens her. She can see something I can't.

"I don't know," I say. "I'm not sure what will happen if we destroy the runabout."

She swallows hard. "I can hazard a guess," she says. "If something explodes in the Boneyard, the Boneyard might think it's being attacked."

"But the thing that explodes would be a ship that's been part of the Boneyard for a long time," I say. "I can't imagine, with all of this equipment, that ships have never exploded inside this place. It might even be a common occurrence."

I'm not sure if I'm speaking out of a weird kind of wishful thinking. But it would seem to me that all this old tech goes wrong on occasion.

Yash is frowning at me. I'm not sure she agrees with me. I'm not sure she knows what she believes.

"We're not a strange vessel to the Boneyard," I continue. "If something explodes near the *Sove*, the Boneyard might simply absorb that explosion."

"Let's assume that's correct," Yash says. "That still won't help us."

It's my turn to frown. "What do you mean?"

"A regular *anacapa* drive will cause all kinds of ripples and energy spikes when it's destroyed. I have no idea what this one will do." She shifts slightly. "I'm not even sure I can predict it."

I nod. Good points all. The bottom line is that we won't know anything at all until we go inside that runabout.

And I've already had a reaction to its malfunctioning *anacapa* drive. If one of my divers reacted as I had, I'm not sure I would allow them inside that runabout.

I'm going to have to come clean before we dive this thing.

Which means I'm going to have to talk to everyone—soon.

9

I SPEND THE NEXT FEW HOURS thinking about the upcoming dive. I pace through part of the *Sove* as I do so, trying to keep myself calm.

Yash's words keep going through my head. There's a lot we don't know here, a lot we need to know.

I'd like to send a probe inside that runabout, but the scans aren't showing any openings a probe can fit through.

We're going to have to explore the exterior of the runabout—or at least pry the doors open to get a probe inside.

My heart is pounding harder just thinking about that, and I suspect, if someone were monitoring me the way that I get monitored the way I do when I'm diving, they would say I have the gids.

I'm too excited about this, and it worries me.

I finally head back to the bridge to see Mikk. He's running some scans from there, just double-checking what we've done. He wants to make sure we didn't miss any other small ships nearby that might have *anacapa* drives.

The bridge is cavernous when it's not fully staffed. Even though four trainees are also working on the bridge, it looks empty. The trainees— two men and two women—are doing something to the equipment. I think I'd have to get closer to understand what they're about. I don't even know these people by name, even though I know we've been introduced.

But I'm not interested in them. I'm interested in Mikk.

He looks odd, his muscular body hunched over a console, his fingers dancing across it. I'm used to seeing Mikk piloting and engaged with exterior views, or diving wrecks himself.

"Can you take a break?" I ask him quietly, but it doesn't matter how low my voice is. The four trainees look up as if I was talking to them.

He nods, and doesn't even glance at them. But I note that he shuts down the program he's running so that they can't see it.

I lead him to the small room off the bridge. When we restored this ship, Coop called that the captain's office, but Yash called it the private meeting room. Neither of them have much use for it.

But Coop runs a different kind of ship than I ever would. I like this room off the bridge, and could see myself using it on all kinds of major dives.

Mikk and I go inside. There's a table and three chairs bolted to the floor. Like most other meeting rooms in the *Sove*, there's also a sideboard so that food and beverages can be served.

Apparently that's an essential part of Fleet culture—the constant appearance of food.

Not that there's any in here. In fact the room's air seems just a little stale, even though I know it's not. The air gets recycled in here as often as it does everywhere else on the ship.

I extend a hand toward the chairs, but Mikk shakes his head just once. He stands so he can see through the clear door. I can opaque the door if I want to, but there's no point.

"Don't tell me," he says. "Yash doesn't believe our readings are right."

"Actually," I say, "she does."

He raises his eyebrows at me in surprise.

I shrug. "That's not the problem."

I tell him what Yash and I discussed, about all the possibilities with the *anacapa* drive in that runabout.

Then I say, "What I want to do is send in a probe, but there are no obvious openings on that runabout. It seems intact."

"We could do a more in-depth scan," he says.

"We could," I say, "and that might still miss an area we could probe. I'd rather do an exterior search."

"And launch the probe from there?"

We've done that a bunch of times in the past.

"Yeah," I say.

He nods, then crosses his arms. "Somehow I don't think that's why you want to see me in private."

I take a deep breath. Time to face the music, both literally and figuratively.

"I need to tell you what happened to me out there," I say.

He extends a hand toward the chairs now. "Should we sit?"

"Probably," I say.

We move to chairs that face each other over the table. I decide to hit the small control that opaques the door after all. I don't want those trainees to see me if this conversation ends up distressing me.

He waits without asking me what's going on. I love that about Mikk. He trusts me to tell him in my own good time.

"When I was on that line," I say, "I heard music."

He nods. He knew that. They all did.

"I thought it beautiful." I let the words hang for a moment, hoping he'll understand.

Something changes in his face. He looks guarded. "Like your mother?"

"Yes," I say quietly. "Or no. I have no idea. I can only guess what she went through."

"But you found that sound alluring," he says.

"Yes," I say.

He sighs. "And you're just telling me now?"

"Yash says that the failing *anacapa* gives off different energy than most malfunctioning *anacapa* drives," I say. "I wonder if that different signal is what I was reacting to."

"Have you discussed this with Orlando and Elaine?" Mikk says.

Ever practical, he's not thinking this is just about me. He's thinking they might have experienced the same thing.

My cheeks grow warm. I hadn't thought of that at all. I was so caught up in my past that I failed to consider the implications for the other divers.

"No," I say.

"We'll need to discuss it with them," he says. "We might not be able to dive this area after all."

"Possibly," I say, even though I don't like that solution. "But I have another idea."

He leans back, his expression even more guarded than before.

"Remember your own rules, Boss," he says. "Safety first. You and I both have seen too many people die on dives."

He helped me with the corpse of one of our old friends, pulling the body out of the Room of Lost Souls after we'd all been lured there on a fake mission. Mikk knows exactly what a malfunctioning *anacapa* drive can do.

"I know we have," I say. I'm trying not to minimize it. "We have two things to consider here. We want material from the Boneyard. It'll help us not just with Lost Souls, but in any battle with the Empire."

Mikk opens his mouth to argue with me, but I don't let him speak, not yet.

"The problem is, as I see it," I say, "that we'll probably encounter malfunctioning *anacapas* and alluring tech like this all over the Boneyard. We all assume that these ships do not work for one reason or another."

He frowns. I know that assumptions aren't always correct. I also know we shouldn't debate that right now.

I continue, "These ships are being stored here, either as a junkyard of damaged ships or as outdated models, maybe to be used for future ships."

"If anyone comes back for them," Mikk says. "Coop believes they were damaged in a battle."

"I know he does." I don't agree with Coop, and I let my tone express that. "Whatever the reason these ships ended up stored here, the problem remains: we're going to encounter more malfunctioning tech. All of it will be dangerous. All of it *is* dangerous."

Mikk shifts his crossed arms, as if trying to make them more comfortable. Or as if he's letting them speak for him.

"You want to dive the Boneyard right here, now, even though you felt lured by that tech," he says.

I nod.

"It's too dangerous, Boss," he says. "You know that. There's nothing you can do to make it safer."

"Yes, there is," I say.

He sighs softly enough that I realize he didn't want me to hear it. I pretend that I didn't hear him.

I say, "We tether to the *Sove* as we dive outside the runabout."

He's shaking his head even as I'm speaking. "We did that, Boss. Remember? At the Room of Lost Souls. The tether didn't work."

It wasn't that the tether didn't work. It got removed—by the diver himself.

"I know," I say. "But I've been thinking about this, and there are some differences."

Mikk taps the fingers of his right hand on his left bicep. I'm not even sure he's aware he's doing it.

"We've already dived the *anacapa* field," I say.

"What?" he asks, clearly surprised. Apparently he had expected me to say something else.

"We were in the energy stream. You were monitoring us through it," I say. "It's different from that time in the Room."

He frowns at me, not entirely understanding.

"When we dove the Room, the diver had to actually go inside the room itself to experience the malfunctioning *anacapa*. The same with that first Dignity Vessel Squishy and I dove."

Where two more of my divers died.

"They entered the field, and *then* had problems. Those fields were hard to access," I say.

Mikk's frown grows deeper.

"Here," I continue, "we've already experienced the field. Maybe not up close, not inside the runabout, exactly, but that's not what we're talking about."

Mikk uncrosses his arms. He's clearly intrigued. "What are we talking about?"

"We're talking about exploring the *exterior*, and then sending in a probe. No closed doors, no secondary area that you can't see. You'll be monitoring our vitals, and you can pull us back if something goes wrong."

He takes a deep breath, clearly thinking about that. He looks away from me, as if looking at me would influence his decision.

Then he turns back toward me, and says slowly, "Before you go on that dive, we're going to review every single second of the aborted dive."

My heart starts racing. I have him. He's agreed.

He knows I'm right. If we're going to dive the Boneyard, we have to face difficulties like this one.

But he's not done with his conditions.

He says, "We're going to figure out if the suits' clocks differ from the *Sove's* clock, down to the nanosecond. We're going to look at your response, in particular, nanosecond by nanosecond. If we find any spike or blip, we're going to examine it."

I want to tell him that it won't be necessary, that we'll be able to handle whatever's going to happen.

But I know better. He's absolutely right. We need information before we go in. We need to be as prepared as possible.

He must have seen the resistance on my face.

"For that reason," he says, "the only people who can do the preliminary dive are you, Orlando, and Elaine."

I let out a small breath. I really want to make this dive. Which concerns me.

"Okay," I say. "Yash might argue with that."

"Let her," he says. "We will have a baseline for comparison on the three of you. We won't have it with her."

He's right. I know he's right.

I nod.

"And one more thing before I completely agree to any of this," he says.

"What's that?" I ask.

"You tell Yash," he says. "*All* of it."

My cheeks heat again. "She doesn't need to know about my family."

"Of course she needs to know about your family," Mikk says. "You're going to do the best you can out there, but you're human, Boss, whether you like to admit it or not. You might get caught by an emotion you haven't considered, something that won't have an impact on Orlando or Elaine or anyone else who dives the Boneyard."

"You're saying I'm the weak link," I say before I can stop myself.

"Yes," he says. "You are."

10

IT TAKES TWO DAYS to prep for the next dive. Yash works side by side with Mikk, giving only a little of the grunt work to Zaria and the trainees. Yash doesn't trust them with anything this important, and frankly, neither do I.

Before the work got underway, I met with Yash, Orlando, and Elaine. I told them about my reaction to the malfunctioning tech, and how it felt different than it had before.

Yash looked at me with concern, and afterwards, she asked me if I thought it was wise to dive the Boneyard, knowing all that. I recognized the verbal ploy. It meant she didn't think I should dive it, and she was urging me to end up in agreement with her.

I didn't change my mind.

Although, after speaking to Orlando and Elaine, I almost decided to do the dive on my own.

Orlando had felt the lure as well. Elaine had too, but apparently she had the capacity to ignore it, which I thought fascinating. None of us were certain as to why there was a difference between Elaine, me, and Orlando, and nothing in the data told us what caused the difference. Her suit was the same as ours. It had the same slightly fluctuating readings as our suits.

The only conclusion I can draw is that she is made of sturdier stuff than Orlando and I. I have always valued Elaine's calm. I'm beginning to think it's an inborn trait, and not something learned. And that calm will help us during this dive.

Yash has repeatedly tried to scan the exterior of that runabout, and find a large enough hole for the probe to enter without us having to make a dive. She couldn't find anything after several tries. She eventually gave that task to the trainees, telling them to be as creative as they could.

She gave them a deadline of this morning to find an alternate way into the runabout.

They couldn't find one.

We're diving it, and I'm trying to ignore the fact that I am a little too happy about that.

11

BY THE AFTERNOON, we're back in the bay. Elaine, Orlando, and I are suited up. My heart is pounding—the damn gids—and I hope I'm not more excited than usual.

Part of me feels more excited than usual.

I focus on the dive. A few hours ago, I made an executive decision. Only two of us would make this particular dive.

I decided the two who would leave the *Sove* are me and Elaine. Elaine's calm is valuable, and will offset my gids.

Orlando would be our reserve diver. If we need rescue—and we might—we need someone who can enter that *anacapa* energy field as safely as Elaine and I can.

Although "safely" is probably the wrong word. I don't know what the actual word would be. The reason I made this decision is pretty simple: We at least have information on Orlando's previous reaction to the field. Any other diver Mikk chooses to rescue us wouldn't have that.

And I've made one other thing clear to the team. Mikk is in charge of this dive. Mikk has been through dangerous *anacapa* situations before. He knows what to do.

More importantly, he knows when to cut our losses and leave.

When I presented this new plan, Yash argued with all of it. But her focus was on me.

"Captains don't go on the most dangerous missions," she said to me.

I shrugged. "I'm not a captain."

Apparently that answer was too flip for her.

"You know what I mean," she said. "The most important person on the team does not take unnecessary risks."

"The most knowledgeable person on the team needs to take these risks at times," I said. "I have the most diving experience, and the most experience in dangerous diving situations."

I didn't add that I also had the most experience of anyone on this ship with malfunctioning *anacapa* drives—malfunctioning stealth tech—and that includes Mikk.

Yash finally figured out that she couldn't sway me. She knew when to stop arguing, which I respected about her.

She also knew that I trusted her to get the entire team back to Lost Souls if something happened to me.

Which it most decidedly will not. I'm doing all I can to make sure that Elaine and I survive this dive.

Mikk and I made a list of everything we had done wrong in previous dives involving what we used to call *stealth tech*. We discussed solutions or ways to avoid all of those problems.

After we had that list in hand, we talked with Yash to see if she had other ideas as well.

She did.

And she had some great work-arounds.

Or I thought they were great until I suited up here in the bay. In addition to the suit, which I'm not really fond of, Elaine, Orlando, and I have attached two tethers to ourselves. Neither tether can be severed by us. They have to be cut off when we return to the ship.

It means we're constantly moving tethers. They are already getting in the way of our movements, which annoys me. Elaine and I will have to be cautious so we don't get caught up in our own lines.

I don't like having extra things to think about, and said so as we were suiting up. Mikk was the one who responded.

He said, *You need something to keep your focus on the dive, Boss. Use the tethers as a mental ground, reminding you that you're diving, not floating in some lovely light.*

The phrase irritated me—still irritates me—but he's right. We need something to remind us that we're part of the *Sove*, not the Boneyard.

The thing that has haunted me the most about my mother's death is that I was with her in that Room. She forgot me. She lost herself in that light and that music, and she forgot I was with her.

I have always given her a pass on that. I have always used that piece of information as an indication of how strong the lure was, that it caused her to abandon her own child.

I need to remember that each time I touch the tethers. I need to remember I can lose myself in beauty that I can only imagine right now.

I try to explain that to Elaine. I think she gets it. It's hard to tell with her sometimes.

We're also attaching the *Sove* to that runabout with an extra strong line. If need be, Yash and Mikk will tow the runabout back to the ship.

I don't want to do that—I don't want the malfunctioning *anacapa* any closer to the *Sove* than it already is—but they say if they end up doing it, it'll only be because I can no longer give orders.

Whatever that means.

I don't think about it much.

I need to focus on the dive. We all need to focus on the dive.

We're nervous. It's pretty clear just from the way we're all behaving. On a normal dive, Orlando, Elaine, and I would suit up alone. This time, Yash is with us, double-checking everything, from the suits to the tethers.

She's spending extra time on the suits, using functions I've never seen. She designed the suits, and apparently, she put in redundant systems.

Normally, I'd be annoyed that she had added things to the design that she hadn't told me about, but on this day, I'm not annoyed at all.

I'm grateful.

Yash is checking everything, from a completely different perspective than Mikk and I bring to this dive.

She's gone over Mikk's findings, the ones that showed us what happened on the previous dive nanosecond by nanosecond.

I went over those readings as well. I know exactly where I heard that music. There was a definite physical change in my suit's readings. It looked like a slightly different version of the gids.

We all marked that.

What bothered me—what still bothers me—is that there was no physical change when I felt the pull of the music the most strongly. When I was hooked by that lure, there was no evidence of it whatsoever.

I'm on my own when it comes to that, and I have promised both Yash and Mikk that I will report any feelings I have that are similar.

I'm hoping there won't be any.

Elaine and I both have probes that we can release into the runabout. If we find an opening, we immediately release a probe, and then signal Mikk and return to the *Sove*.

That's the plan we all hope will work. We all doubt that it will, however.

Elaine and I also have levers attached to our belts so that we can pull the runabout's doors open by hand, if need be. Yash has given us her passcodes to Fleet ships, but I doubt the codes will work.

I suspect this vessel is thousands of years newer than the *Ivoire*. I'm sure that entry passcodes have changed in the intervening centuries.

But I don't say that to Yash, particularly after she has impressed on me, for the third time, that I should try the codes first if we don't find any other entry point.

Mikk is nowhere near the bay. He's on the bridge, where he's going to monitor everything that we do. He's already got the previous dive data on the screens before him.

Mikk has already told me that I am a little too giddy, but he's careful in his word choice. He did not say that I have the gids.

And when Yash asked if my readings are different than they were before the previous dive, Mikk said they are.

Apparently, I'm calmer.

Which is a relief to me, because I feel calmer. I feel like I know what we're getting into. I feel like I am going into this dive as prepared as I can possibly be.

Elaine doesn't say much. She doesn't look nervous either, but then she never does before a dive.

Yash finishes, giving us one more lecture, and checking the tethers one last time.

Then she leaves the bay.

Elaine and I put our hoods on, and double-check each other's. Orlando puts his on as well.

He's going to wait down here until we're done, monitoring everything.

I give the order to have the bay's environmental system shut off—not the gravity, but the earth-like oxygen mix.

We use the oxygen mix as our baseline for the suits. If the suits have some kind of leak, we will learn about it while we're inside the *Sove*, not outside and already at risk.

We breathe in. We breathe out. Everything registers as normal.

"You ready?" I ask Elaine.

She doesn't give me a cute or flip answer, which I appreciate.

"I am ready," she says.

"Well, then," I say. "Let's go."

12

ON MY COMMAND, the bay doors slide open. I go out first, gripping the line between the *Sove* and the runabout with my left hand. It feels odd to travel with two other tethers attached to my suit. They float around me like loose coils on a badly designed ship. I have to ignore them as I move, ignore them while making certain that they do not trap me.

Already I can hear the siren song of the malfunctioning *anacapa* drive. It's not a full-blown chorus yet. More like voices heard underwater.

I grip the line, and wait for Elaine to exit.

She shoves at her other tethers as well; clearly, they bother her as much as they bother me.

Then she nods, and we start forward.

We have allotted ninety minutes for this dive. That's longer than a standard dive, but we've all agreed that it's better to make one long dive than make several short ones.

It helps that the runabout is much closer to the *Sove* than the other Dignity Vessel is.

I'm moving toward the runabout, hand over hand, going slowly, keeping my breathing even. It must be working, because Mikk confirms that I'm still not nearly as giddy as I was on that first dive.

Elaine and I take turns reporting on what we hear.

She doesn't seem to have the same kind of reaction that I have to the *anacapa* energy swirling around us. I hear faint voices before she does, and then I hear full harmony, as if those voices have worked their way into a crescendo.

At that point, she just starts hearing those voices.

As I get closer to the runabout, I hear even more voices. Full-fledged choral music, running up and down the diatonic scale, just like before.

Elaine can't hear the runs. She only hears the voices, growing louder.

I try not to think about those differences. I need to focus on the dive itself.

As we move forward, I survey everything around us.

I'm still hoping to see smaller bits of ships, something else that might be causing this energy field.

I'm not seeing anything new, though. The same fighters, an orbiter, and the runabout, all in the shadow—so to speak—of the Dignity Vessel, which is off to my left.

Far above us, the Boneyard's force field glistens ever so slightly. Yash thinks the glistening is a weak area, which makes sense to me, if there's a strong malfunctioning *anacapa* field.

Although I also consider that hypothesis to be just that—a theory, something we haven't tested yet.

I pull myself closer to the runabout. We're not far from it now.

Deeper voices add into the music, also singing in identical chords, pure and strong. The voices provide a much-needed baseline. And, for the first time, I hear myself mentally call that music beautiful.

Before Mikk can comment on that, I make note of it, and my heart starts pounding hard. Now, we might get to the moment where they pull me back.

I don't want to go back. I want to finish this dive.

I check in with myself, though. I need to make sure that I want to finish this dive because of the dive itself, not because I'm feeling drawn toward the runabout.

The thought calms me down, makes me feel more like myself. There's a place I go to inside myself, a place I'm very familiar with but is hard to get to. It's as if I wrap my personality inside a shell, which exists inside my body.

I use this place most often on dangerous dives. I've trained it, with the hopes that it will appear when I need it. Sometimes it doesn't—not in situations outside of diving.

But in dives, it does.

And it has.

And that fills me with just a little relief.

I don't let my guard down though. I find that I can focus better, though. I no longer worry about Elaine. It's her job to track her own reactions, and Mikk's job to assess whether or not she needs to be removed.

My job is to examine the exterior of that runabout, and get a probe inside it.

It takes only ten minutes of very slow going to reach the runabout. The line has dug into the runabout's side just below the main entry doors, which is not something we intended. But the entrance faces the *Sove*, which is a point that works in our favor.

The music is loud here, crashingly loud. It makes my head ache.

I no longer consider it beautiful. Now it's as annoying as an unknown neighbor in my old apartment building on Hector Prime who played his music so loud that it echoed through the entire building, no matter how the rest of us set our apartments' privacy settings.

My suit shakes from the music—or it seems to—and it feels like the beat has invaded my skin.

I report that to Mikk, then ask if my heart rate has elevated.

"No," he says curtly. All of his responses have been curt, as if I'm bothering him every time I speak.

I know that's a sign that he's concentrating, and I try not to worry about it. But usually he's more talkative when he's in charge of a dive—even a dicey one like this.

"I'm feeling it too," Elaine says. "It's as if something is crawling on my skin, but to a musical beat."

"Weird." That comment, faint but pointed, comes from Yash. She apparently has looped into our comm. I don't entirely appreciate that, but it's too late to change now.

The music is starting to give me a headache in my forehead, just above my eyes. I report that as well, but I get no real response from Mikk. I don't expect one.

He's probably making certain that the environmental systems in my suit are working properly, and there's not another reason for the headache.

I check the oxygen mix, just to make sure. It's normal. According to all the readings on my suit, everything on the interior is exactly like it was when we left the *Sove*.

I take a deep breath. The air has a slightly metallic taste, which is normal for these suits, and I focus on that.

Normal.

Then I lean forward and put my right glove on the runabout.

My glove has sensors everywhere. It automatically sends readings back to the *Sove*. Mikk won't tell me what those readings say unless I specifically ask or unless something in them puts me in danger.

I keep my left hand on the main line to the *Sove*, at least for the moment, giving Mikk a minute to record all of this information and maybe tell me to abort. He still says nothing.

Elaine reaches my side, and mimics my action, only keeping her right hand on the line, and placing her left glove on the side of the runabout.

We both look around.

The perspective here is different: I can feel the rest of the Boneyard around me, but it also seems far away. The only important ship is the one I'm nose to nose with.

The runabout's side is badly pockmarked and gray with age. This is a decay I recognize. I've seen it in the ancient sector bases that I traveled to with Coop. I've seen it at the Room of Lost Souls. I have no idea if the information from my glove will reinforce this, but my eyes tell me that this runabout isn't just damaged, it's thousands of years old.

Some nanobits slough off the side near my right hand. It almost feels like I activated a small storm of bits when I touched the runabout. Tiny tiny particles float past me and into the space around me. They'll be on the suit when I return, just like they'll be on Elaine's.

I look over at her. She's also in a small cloud of bits.

The side of the runabout feels flimsy. Parts of it have clearly been sloughing off for a very long time now.

Aside from the pockmarks, I see no holes on this part of the runabout. Elaine is examining her side as well.

"Anything?" I ask.

"Lots of damage," she says, "but time did this, not some other ship."

I agree.

"There might be something off to my right," she says. "I'm going that way."

"We're going together," I say. This dive is too dangerous to separate, even for a few minutes.

I keep my left hand on the line, then slowly sink below it. That will also give me a view of the underside of this runabout—or what passes for the underside, given our perspective.

The part of the underside that I see has the same kind of pockmarking. I have no idea how thick the hull of a runabout should be, but this just looks flimsy to me. Thin.

I touch it, and it almost feels as if I can shove my hand through it.

I don't, of course. The last thing I want to do is cut my suit.

And I don't want to use a laser pistol or any kind of weaponry out here to open the runabout, if we can avoid it.

I duck under the line and ease my way to Elaine's side. The bad thing about going this direction is that she will be first, not me. I hadn't thought that through when we made the decision, and that bothers me.

I feel focused, but I'm also aware that part of my brain is now coping with the headache. It hasn't grown worse, but it's there, strong and powerful. My teeth ache. I move my jaw just a little to make sure I'm not grinding my teeth together.

I'm not.

But I can feel that music in my bones.

I pull myself up so that my head reaches Elaine's waist.

"I'm going to stay low," I say.

"I'll move up," she says in response.

We can cover more ground this way. The runabout isn't that big, not like a Dignity Vessel. We couldn't go all the way around a Dignity Vessel on one dive. But we should be able to see the entire exterior of the runabout, launch the probe, and get back long before our ninety-minute window.

We've only been out here for fifteen minutes so far, although with this pounding in my head, it feels longer.

Then that thought registers. I say, "Mikk, how long have we been here according to the *Sove?*"

"Fifteen minutes, eighteen seconds," he says.

It matches the reading in my suit exactly.

"That's what I have," I say.

"Me, too," Elaine says.

Good news then. So far, Yash's suits are working better next to the runabout than they had on the line.

Elaine has let go of the line. Both of her hands are gripping the side of the runabout, using some kind of adhering technology that is Fleet-made, not the half-assed stuff I used to use. She also finds handholds and props her boots against the side of the runabout, probably in deference to me.

My feet dangle because there's no runabout below my thighs. I hang onto the side of the runabout as tightly as I can, and still allow my gloves to register something.

The pockmarks remain consistent as we move along the side.

"I've got something," Elaine says, "but it doesn't go all the way through. This little ship took some fire once upon a time."

She reaches up, and puts her hand in a groove that I can see from below. As we move slowly around the side of the runabout, the groove becomes apparent to me as well.

Something shot at this runabout, probably with a laser weapon, but didn't penetrate the hull. I raise myself just a little so that I'm face-to-face with the bottom of the scoring. If there's a small hole here, we might be able to use one of our tools to make it a larger hole.

But it looks like the damage occurred long enough ago that the nanobits repaired the injury to the side of the runabout as the damage happened. They apparently did not have the strength or the numbers to replicate well enough to make the damage go away entirely.

Either that, or the hull is thicker than I expected.

As we move to the side of the runabout, I glance over my shoulder. Small ships that I had only seen as holoimages inside a three-dimensional map in the *Sove* hover behind me. They look bigger than I expected them to be.

And they're canted at odd angles, so they actually look like they're moving just a little. Or like they've been frozen in the midst of some kind of battle.

Moving my head enough to look at those ships has eased my headache somewhat. Then I realize it's not cause and effect. The headache eased when I moved to this side of the runabout.

The headache didn't entirely go away, but the music seems a lot less loud.

"Has the music changed for you, Elaine?" I ask.

"Yeah," she says. "It's softer. Although I'm not sure you can use the word 'soft' for this stuff."

She's right about that. It's less intense.

"My head feels a bit better as well," she says.

"Mine, too," I tell her.

We keep going, examining the side closely. I'm not seeing holes, and Elaine isn't saying that she is either. Occasionally, when she moves her hands, more nanobits come off the vessel.

Since I'm holding on to the scored groove in the runabout, nothing is coming off here. It's also darker than the part that Elaine's touching, which leads me to believe that this injury to the side of the runabout happened after it had been abandoned, lost, floating—something—for some time, but before it got so old that the exterior started coming apart.

I'm sure the readings from my gloves will give us more information on that.

Every few meters, I duck down and look underneath the runabout. So far, I'm not seeing any holes there either, and no more examples of some kind of laser fire. At some point, one of us will have to look at the part of the runabout that we're now calling the top, even though it's not the top of the runabout. Like everything else we see, it's slightly canted.

Faint swirls mark doors that open when the regular engine is in use. Attached to the one area near my feet is the bubble in the hull that marks an escape pod tube. The tube is closed, which means the pod was never used.

Had the pod been used, the tube would have had an opening on at least one side.

Elaine keeps moving, hand over hand, and starts to turn the corner to the back side of the runabout.

"No," Mikk says. He sounds more forceful than I'm used to hearing from him. "You can't go around that side. I need to be able to see you. Both of you."

"We'll be fine," Elaine says, knowing he's talking to her. "There's a lot to cover—"

"No," I say. "Mikk's right. We don't go on that side."

"But—" Elaine starts, then stops herself. She knows better than to argue with the people in charge of the dive. I hear her sigh. "You can't see much when you're looking at us, Mikk. Just monitor us on the equipment."

"*No,*" he says so forcefully that it startles me. I don't recognize the tone in his voice, but I understand it.

Mikk is frightened—and rightfully so. Everyone who has died in these malfunctioning *anacapa* areas on our watch has done so when we couldn't see them.

"You will *not* be out of my range of sight. Or we *will* end this mission right now." He's moving from forceful to a tinge of panic.

"Boss," Elaine says to me, turning slightly. "Tell him—"

"He's right, Elaine. If we don't find anything on the sides he can see, we'll send a probe around the back." I'm saying that to mollify her. When the time comes, I won't authorize a probe around that side of the runabout. That's just a waste of a probe. Instead, we'll pry those doors.

"All right," she says, but she sounds skeptical. "Can I at least make my way back to the front across the top of this thing?"

I don't know if she's asking me or if she's asking Mikk. But I'm going to let him answer her.

"Only if you climb up there from the place Boss is right now," he says to Elaine. "I'll be able to see you if you do that."

"All right," she says.

I start to move back the way I came. I'm putting my hands on the spots I used before. I am not going to go completely underneath this vessel, and I note that Mikk didn't suggest it. He seems worried about Elaine, and frankly, I am as well.

It's not like her to question what the leader of a dive says.

I move out of her way far enough that she pulls herself to the top of the runabout—or what's passing for the top here. I pull myself up higher too, placing my gloved hands just above the holds she originally used. I also brace my boots on the sides.

I can feel slight vibrations as she pulls herself along the top of this runabout. Or maybe those vibrations are from the energy causing that music. I don't know, and it's not for me to figure out.

But the music has receded, at least on this side of the runabout, to the levels I've experienced before in the Boneyard.

My headache remains but it isn't all encompassing.

We make our way back to the side of the runabout facing the *Sove*. Elaine reaches that part of the runabout first, and waits for me. I make my way around.

"There's nothing up here," she says.

The music grows stronger the closer I get to our original line. I peer at it, then at the Dignity Vessel we were initially going to dive. Am I wrong? Is the malfunctioning *anacapa* on that vessel?

I'm about to tell Mikk that the music is loud once again when Elaine speaks up.

She says, "Hey, Boss, we might have something here."

13

I CLIMB UP JUST A BIT FARTHER, careful that my extra tethers don't get caught in the line between the *Sove* and the runabout. Elaine keeps one hand and both feet on the runabout, but points at the side we haven't examined yet.

She found something there.

Strangely, I'm not excited about that.

"I'll look," I say.

I straddle the door, then return to the part of the runabout I initially attached to.

Then I work my way around to the area that Elaine is pointing at. Once I get close, she eases herself over the edge, making sure her tethers stay in place as well.

There's a hole to the right of the second escape pod tube. The hole is larger than I would have thought, but dark, like the nanobits had started to repair it.

I turn on the light on the back of my glove and aim it at the hole. I see some ragged edges, which I don't like, and then I note that they've smoothed out just a bit, farther in.

The hole is wide enough that, if I move closer, I can stick my fist in there, and still see around it to see if it opens to the inside.

I can do that without touching any of the jagged edges if I go slowly enough.

The music has gotten very, very loud here, bad enough that my eyes actually water from the pain.

I tell Mikk about the music. Then I ask, "How long have we been on this dive?"

"Thirty-three minutes, nine seconds," he says, sounding concerned.

My suit tells me we've been here thirty-three minutes, eight seconds. It's not a big enough discrepancy to make me stop.

I'm going to investigate this hole, and then I'll ask him the time again. This time, I'll tell him that our clocks have slide out of sync.

If he doesn't already know that.

I stick my fist inside, the light catching the entire interior. The blackness gleams at me from the back side of that hole.

"The nanobits have done their job," Yash says in my ear. She sounds dispirited. "They closed the hole. Looks like they didn't have enough strength to repair it entirely, but they managed to keep the runabout intact."

I want to ask her when she thought this happened, how far along in this runabout's clearly long and tortured history, but I'll wait to ask that question until I'm back inside the *Sove*.

Elaine has floated down beside me, still holding the runabout with one hand. I ask her to check the hole from her side.

She peers inside, then shines two lights in there, one from her hood and one from her glove. After a moment, she shakes her head.

"The nanobits closed it off," she says, "if it ever got breached."

I let out a sigh, knowing Mikk will pick up on my frustration. I don't care. If we could go around the back side, the side he can't see easily, then we might find another hole.

But it looks like the nanobits put their last scrap of energy into repairing the hull from whatever attacked it. If we find a hole back there, odds are that it too will be partially repaired.

"You up for trying the doors?" I ask her. We've been out here, according to my suit's clock, for forty minutes.

"Yes," she says. She doesn't sound tired, but perhaps I'm simply reading that into her response.

As we work our way back to the runabout's main doors, I check our clock with Mikk. We're still one second different. I tell him that, and he makes note.

We're nearly to the doors, when Yash says, "Remember the—" before something or someone (probably Mikk) cuts her off. I don't say anything to reassure her. Of course we'll try the passcodes first. We've been lucky in the past. Some of the ancient and abandoned sector bases that we discovered used the passcodes Yash and Coop were familiar with.

But I'm convinced that even though this runabout is ancient, it's not *that* ancient. She's going to be disappointed, but there's nothing I can do about that.

I reach the doors first, and raise myself over the line so that I'm on the far side. I have to move my tethers again. Even though they were my idea, I hate them. They're awkward and in the way.

Elaine is close behind me. We both scan the sides—all four of them—around the door, looking for the area where the exterior panel would be.

I don't see one, and neither does Elaine. We switch sides, and search again.

Even with the flaking nanobits and the thin hull, I'm not seeing anything that suggests a control panel. I move to the center of the door closest to me and run my glove over it. I toggle my faceplate so that I can see the readings, but according to the data streaming along one side, there's no difference on the surface, nothing that would suggest an exterior access.

"Yash," I say into the comm, "the Fleet wouldn't build a runabout without a way to access it from the outside, would they?"

After I ask the question, I wince. I know how she's going to respond: *They wouldn't build a runabout with an anacapa drive either, Boss, but they did.*

To my surprise, she doesn't say that. She says, "They might, especially for use in hostile areas. They might have built the doors to respond to a bit of equipment that the pilot carries with himself or something."

"Remote access," I say. "You wouldn't have any idea how to replicate that, would you?"

"Right now? While you're diving? No." She sounds vaguely amused, as if I have imbued her with powers beyond those a human being might have. "Maybe if you come back, I might be able to rig up something that has a—oh, I don't know—twenty percent chance of working."

Not good enough, and we both know it.

"You up for prying the doors?" I ask Elaine.

"Yes," she says.

It's dangerous. We have to be careful to make sure our suits don't snag or get ripped. We also need to attach ourselves to the runabout itself so that we can have our hands free.

And it will take a lot of physical strength to lever the doors open because we don't have anything to brace against. Gravity might work against us in this circumstance, but it might also work for us.

And if I had to bet, I would bet that we'd do better in gravity. We're used to it.

But I don't say that to Elaine. Instead, I say, "All we need is to open it a few centimeters so we can shove the probe inside."

"What if there's an airlock?" she asks.

She's right. I hadn't planned for the airlock.

"All right," I concede. "Maybe half a meter or so. I should be able to squeeze through that."

Because there's no chance that the airlock will be automated.

I think.

Elaine doesn't argue with me about squeezing through. I half expect Mikk or Yash to say something, but neither of them do as well.

I'm hoping that's because they agree with what we plan, not because the time has slipped yet again.

Elaine and I use grapplers built into the sides of our suits to tether ourselves to the crumbling nanobit pockmarks on the runabout. The grapplers claw into the sides just enough to keep us in place. We also use our boots to adhere to the side of the runabout, leaving our arms free.

I debate tethering ourselves to the line as well, but we already have extra tethers hooking us to the *Sove*, and that should be enough.

The music whoops and dives, less of a chorus right here than a raucous, atonal symphony. For some reason, that bothers me less than the choral music did.

The headache remains, but it is less important now.

I take out my lever, and place it in the very thin line between the two entrance doors. From what I can tell, the doors are designed to slide into the hull.

Elaine does the same thing from her side. We double-check each other, and agree to pull at the count of three.

I'm the one who counts.

Then we pull.

For long, agonizing seconds, the doors don't budge. Then hers jiggles just a little. All we need is one, but I'm not giving up on mine.

It appears to be stuck, though.

She keeps pulling. If she's putting as much effort into this as I am, then she's sweating inside that suit, no matter what the environmental controls are doing.

Her door jumps a bit more, then pulls back nearly a full meter.

That's all we need.

"Good," I say.

"I can go in," she says.

"No," I say, bracing myself for another one of those *you're the most important person* arguments. But she doesn't make it and neither does Yash.

I use the lever to pull myself closer to the doors. A meter is more than wide enough for me to slide inside sideways, and I do.

The nanobits are floating in here as well, just as disturbed as they are outside the runabout. The music is even louder. Deafening doesn't begin to describe it. All-consuming, maybe. I'm beginning to wonder if that sound—that energy—whatever it is—is doing some kind of damage to my brain or my body.

But I can't worry about that.

There is an airlock, just like Elaine predicted there would be. If I had been thinking clearly, I would have known it too. This headache, the music, they're all interfering with my thought processes. I need to get the probe into the runabout, and then Elaine and I need to get back to the *Sove* as fast as possible.

I slide into the airlock and as I get inside, I realize that Mikk can't see me. A shiver runs down my back. Was this what my divers experienced when they died? Headaches? Loud music? An inability to focus?

Whatever it is, I can't afford to worry about it now.

I have to get the airlock door open, and push the probe through it.

First, I place my gloved hand on the airlock door. It's an old failsafe system that Coop told me about for any drifting Fleet ship. Figuring that a drifting ship is a ship without power, there's a physical mechanism, an actual mechanical weight system inside the door that's activated by the kind of slap caused by a human hand at just the right level.

The mechanism exists on the airlock's interior door, not an exterior door. The theory is, according to Coop, that only members of the Fleet would know this trick. And no one would want an accidental activation on the outside of any kind of ship.

I don't expect this glove-slap to work. I'm not sure the Fleet would have left something mechanical in their ships. I assume that the ships, large and small, have evolved tremendously since Coop's time.

But the door in front of me wobbles. Then it shakes a little, and opens maybe half a centimeter. That's all I need. I insert the lever, brace my feet against the wall, and pull.

This door opens easily.

There's darkness beyond and even louder music.

My hand shakes as I grab the probe from my belt. I activate the probe and toss it inside.

I wonder if I should send one more after it, then realize that the doors probably won't close. We will have an easy time sending another probe into that darkness. We can do it from the *Sove*.

If I can get back to the *Sove*. My eyes are watering from the pain in my head. I grip the exterior door with the hand not holding the lever, and propel myself out of the runabout.

I use so much strength that I vault past Elaine, past the line, and into the emptiness of space between all of the ships. I'm going to have to use those damn tethers to pull myself back to the *Sove*.

I haven't made a mistake like this since I was on my earliest training dives. I'm better than this. I'm—

The music is softening. I swallow, the pain inside my head easing just a bit.

"Boss? You okay?" That's Mikk, I think, talking in my ear.

"I think," I manage, and I hope to hell I'm speaking aloud, "Elaine and I are going to need help returning to the *Sove*."

I'm gripping the tether, trying to remember how to use it to get myself to the *Sove*. One hand over the other, sending tether behind me, right?

And then the tether becomes tense. It pulls against my waist. I can feel it through the suit.

I'm zipping through the wide open emptiness faster than I've ever moved on my own in space. I should look for Elaine, but I don't want to move my head. I don't want the pain to return. I don't want….

14

I WAKE UP IN A BED. I have no idea how I've gotten here. For a moment, I wonder if it's an hallucination.

I try to stand up, but I'm so dizzy that I can't lift my head upright.

I haven't seen this room before. It's brightly lit, with comforting pale blue walls. The bed is softer than any I've ever been on before.

I lie down and as I do, I notice that my arms are shaking.

I have no idea if I'm imagining this. But if I am, I am at least imagining a better place than the one I left.

At least there's blessed silence here.

Or there is, until the sound of a door scraping open makes my skin crawl.

The med tech we've brought on this trip, who serves in the Fleet and whose name I have forgotten, fills the doorway. She's short and cheerful and too damn young to know anything about medicine.

Or maybe I'm too damn cranky.

All I know is she's not a full-fledged doctor. She's been a tech forever and then she decided to move up in medicine. I'm pretty sure she doesn't even know what she doesn't know.

Or something like that.

My head doesn't hurt, but my brain feels slower than usual. It feels like I'm forming thoughts through clouds.

And one of the thoughts that finally makes it through the damp grayness is that if the med tech is here, then we're still on the *Sove*.

She comes all the way into the room, holding one of those medical pads that we have on every level of this ship. Anyone can diagnose the simple stuff programmed into that pad, and maybe perform treatments, also programmed in. We figured having a human for the exotic stuff was one step up.

Stuff. God, I can't even come up with words properly.

She smiles at me, and I feel helpless. I can't get away from a person I don't know who is grinning at me. It makes me nervous.

Then the door scrapes farther, and Yash enters the room.

I'm not sure if that's better or worse.

She actually smiles when she sees me. She never does that.

"You're awake!" She sounds surprised.

It takes me a moment to remember the transition. I had been in my suit, hearing music so strong that I was in a kind of pain I'd never experienced—and now I'm here, wearing some silky pajamas, lying between soft sheets on an even softer bed.

"Elaine?" I manage. My voice sounds old and dry.

Yash's smile fades. The med tech looks at her, expecting Yash to say whatever it is that needs to be said.

I want to close my eyes against the news. Elaine is dead. I've killed another diver by being reckless, by ignoring the warnings about stealth tech/*anacapa* drives. I've—

"She's in a healing coma," the med tech says. "We're bringing her out slowly."

It takes a moment for the words to register because I'd been so braced for the news that she had died.

"Healing…?" I ask.

"We did the same with you," the med tech says. "You passed out on the dive. We woke you briefly—do you remember?"

Those damn mental clouds. I focus, grope for memories, find… some light, voices, hands grappling at my hood, Mikk saying *You're not doing this to me, Boss. You're not*…and then nothing.

"I'm not sure," I say.

"That's normal," the tech says, tapping that pad just a little. I have no idea if she's looking up what's normal for this situation or if she actually knows that it's normal. I'm beginning to worry that she doesn't know.

"It doesn't matter," Yash says curtly. "You're conscious now. How are you feeling?"

"Shaky," I say, because there's no point in lying. "Was I injured?"

Yash presses her lips together. The med tech brings down her pad, and looks at me for a moment.

God help me, I recognize that look. It's an evaluation of the person on the other side of the conversation. There's a calculation that goes into it: *Is she capable of understanding what I'm going to say? Is she emotionally ready to hear it? Do I lie? Do I lie now and tell the truth later? Do I lie forever?*

"Yes," the med tech says after a moment. "There was damage on a cellular level. After some discussion, we decided to use a nanorepair kit on both you and Elaine, in conjunction with the medically induced coma."

So many questions. I'm having trouble sorting them. So I decide to stop. I'll ask as they come up.

"Why didn't we go back to Lost Souls?" I ask.

Yash hadn't wanted us to dive in the first place. She had wanted us to leave. So the logical thing to do, with two members of this relatively small crew injured, would have been to make sure we were all right. Return to Lost Souls, then dive later.

Even I would have approved that.

"It's too risky to activate our *anacapa* drive," Yash says.

I feel cold despite all of the covers and the proper settings for the environmental system.

I start to sit up, but the med tech puts her warm hand on my shoulder.

"Stay still," she says. Then she looks at Yash. "We can discuss this later."

"Not if you want me to stay in bed," I say. "We're discussing this now."

"See?" Yash says to her. "I told you she would have questions you can't answer."

Yash sits on the side of the bed so that I'm not looking up at her. I actually appreciate that. I hadn't realized how much effort it took just to tilt my head.

"Before you ask," she says, "we don't know exactly what happened."

"To me and Elaine? Or to the runabout? Or to the *Sove?*" I ask.

"The *Sove* is fine," Yash says. "Nothing happened to this ship at all."

"Then why can't we use our *anacapa* drive?" I ask.

She takes a deep breath, then folds her hands together as if she's keeping them from trembling.

"Because," she says, "we don't know what'll happen to the Boneyard if we do."

15

<small>WHAT SHE TELLS ME IS THIS:</small>

The readings from that malfunctioning *anacapa* drive spiked after we opened the airlock door. Right now, Yash and Mikk have no idea why. The probe went in and did send information back, but they haven't processed it yet.

Yash and Mikk want to do it themselves, but they haven't had time. Instead, they've been helping care for me and Elaine.

"How long have we been down?" I ask, frustrated that even asking a simple question is harder than I want it to be.

"Only twelve hours," Yash says. "Jaylene wanted us to feed this information to you slowly, but I knew you wouldn't accept that."

"That's right," I say.

She nods and continues, with Jaylene the med tech hovering.

"When the readings spiked," Yash says, "Mikk asked you if you were all right."

I remember that clearly. His voice, breaking through the music, like a lifeline.

"I told him we'd need help getting back," I say, frowning at the ache that accompanied the memory. Not an emotional ache. An ache inside my brain.

"Yes," Yash says, "you did. But it was odd. Your words reached him after we had already started tugging you toward the *Sove*."

The time differential. Apparently it had gotten worse.

"We got you and Elaine at the same time. Then we unhooked the line that attached the *Sove* to the runabout. We thought about leaving, but…."

Yash just stops talking, as if she's censoring herself. I squirm, ready to sit up again. Jaylene, the med tech, presses on my shoulder ever so gently. This woman is not going to let me up without a fight.

"But?" I demand.

"It stopped," Yash says.

I'm worried that my brain didn't process what she said correctly. "What stopped?"

"The energy from that malfunctioning *anacapa*," she says. "We're getting no readings from it at all."

"Is it our equipment?" I ask.

Yash gives me a withering look.

"I'm not asking as if you haven't done your job," I say, understanding the look. "I'm trying to understand."

She nods, and I suddenly realize that she's exhausted. The last eighteen hours or so have taken a toll on her.

"We have checked, double-checked, and triple-checked the equipment," she says. "We thought of launching another probe, but we haven't had time. I don't want the trainees to do it."

I understand that.

"The energy is just not registering at the moment," Yash says.

"And the probe?" I ask.

"Still sending information," she says. "We're not getting readings about the malfunctioning drive from the probe either."

I lean back on the pillow. Jaylene's hand moves with me. This woman does not trust me at all.

She shouldn't. If she and Yash weren't so insistent, I'd be up and moving around.

"So," I say, "what's the plan?"

"We're going to wait," Yash says. "As soon as you're able, we'll watch the footage from the probe. We're analyzing the data now."

"And if I'm not able?" I ask. The words feel odd, but then, so do I. And while we've been discussing the ships and the crew, we haven't really discussed what's going on with me.

Yash sighs as if she had hoped I wasn't going to ask that question. She glances at Jaylene to see if Jaylene wants to take the question.

Apparently, Jaylene doesn't.

"Then we'll have to leave the Boneyard," Yash says.

Her words hang. She expects me to understand something. I'm waiting for the clouds to part, but they don't.

So I have to ask.

"How?"

"We'll cut a hole in the force field surrounding it, like we did before with that skip," she says. "We'll exit the Boneyard, and then we'll activate our *anacapa*."

It takes a second for the thoughts to process. "You're afraid that the Boneyard will fire on us again," I say.

"Yes." Her answer is curt. "We have no idea what the firepower of the Boneyard itself is. But if it harnesses the firepower of many of its ships, then I'm not sure we can fight it."

I lean my head back. Just this little discussion is tiring me out. What the hell happened to me out there? I've never felt like this before.

"We have to find out what's going on with that *anacapa* drive, Boss," Yash says. "We have to know if that flare was the last gasp of the *anacapa* or if we triggered something when we opened that door. We need to know what kind of danger we're in."

"We can't dive it again," I say.

"We don't know that," Yash says. "If the *anacapa* drive is dead, we can easily dive it."

I can't believe I'm on the other side of this argument for once.

"We still won't know if it's safe," I say.

Jaylene moves, turning her body so that I can't see her face. But I know what she's doing. She's telling Yash to back off.

Which is probably smart. Because I'm feeling distressed, and being distressed actually hurts.

"We have time to decide this," Yash says.

"Before we do," I say, "let's double-check the original readings."

Yash frowns at me. "What do you mean?"

"Mikk and I were convinced the runabout's *anacapa* was the one malfunctioning. But as I moved around that runabout's exterior, the energy—the sound—faded. If it was the runabout, should it have done that?"

"That's the problem," Yash says. "It shouldn't have done any of this."

16

After that, Jaylene makes Yash leave. Jaylene doesn't want Yash to tire me out. But Jaylene stays. She takes her hand off my arm, and she uses the bed's diagnostic system to run some tests.

She tells me only part of the results, and I'm getting so fatigued, I'm not sure I care.

But I do care about one thing. After she finishes running her tests, I ask, "Tell me exactly. What kind of damage did that little adventure do to me?"

Her gaze flicks toward the door, as if she's been instructed not to talk to me like this without Yash present.

But Yash isn't in charge of this mission, I am. Although Yash is the senior Fleet officer on board.

I'm going to ignore that detail, though. It's my body. My health.

"According to Mikk," Jaylene says, "everyone who has died in a malfunctioning *anacapa* field like the one you encountered aged prematurely."

"Not exactly," I say. "They mummified."

"And the suits registered that they had been in the *anacapa* field much longer than they actually had by our calculations," Jaylene said.

"Yes," I say. "We measured hours. Their bodies measured years."

"So it looked like aging." She's pushing this for a reason.

"I'm not sure he explained that clearly to you," I say. "Did you look at the records?"

"I will," she says. "I've been busy with the two of you."

She means me and Elaine, not me and Mikk.

"The point is," Jaylene says, "that those victims who died in malfunctioning *anacapa* fields, they had been destroyed on a cellular level, in ways consistent with time passing."

Apparently, she confuses that with aging. But I'll give her that.

"More or less," I say, unable to give her a full yes.

"You've been able to tolerate malfunctioning *anacapa* fields in the past," she says.

It's not a question, but I answer as if it were one. "Yes."

"And you were doing fine in this malfunctioning *anacapa* field until the very end," she says.

"Yash says the energy was higher than she'd ever seen it," I say.

"Yes, it was." Jaylene taps the pad in front of her. Then she turns it toward me. A round, gelatinous object faces me. It almost looks like a planet, surrounded by a watery ring. Something about it pleases me, like staring into deep space pleases me.

Then she taps the screen, and shows me a similar object. It's gray now, and most of the liquid appears to be gone. The central "planet" isn't round any longer. It's flat on the sides, and bits of it are flaking off into the liquid. It reminds me, in some ways, of the graying nanobits that we encounter on aging ships.

"These are two versions of your cells," Jaylene says. "The first came from your last exam, just before we left on this voyage. The second was what your cells looked like when you returned from your dive."

My stomach tightens. My mouth has gone dry.

Then she taps the screen again. Now I know what I'm looking at, kinda. Something black and round, even smaller than the cell itself, seems to be rounding up the flakes and piling them together. The cell isn't quite as gray.

"That's one of your cells six hours ago," she says, "after we injected you with the nanobits. I just took one more scan…"

She taps the screen again, and now the flakes are gone. The cell isn't gray but it isn't entirely healthy either, although it's getting its shape back.

The nanothingies, whatever they are, seem focused away from the center, and are congregating near the edge.

"That's what the cell looks like right now," she says. "It's improving. But I have no idea how long the improvement will take, if it will bring you back to normal for you, or if it will last."

Well, that was brutal. I don't say that, of course. But I'm feeling woozy, and that's partly because I've been holding my breath throughout her entire presentation.

"So, on the health question," she says, "I have no idea what a full recovery will be for you. Clearly, this is something we've just discovered, and it's going to take a lot of work examining it, and figuring out what caused it."

"But you believe this is what happened to my other divers," I say.

"Yes," she says, "and contrary to what Mikk told me, it seems to happen rapidly, not slowly. The outside force attacks each cell, sucking it of its life in one way or another."

"Or its moisture," I say, thinking about what I considered liquid.

She shrugs one shoulder. "Perhaps. We don't know. And this kind of study is outside of my expertise."

"Is this what happened everywhere?" I ask. And then I force myself to amend the question. "Even in my brain?"

"The brain is a web of connective tissue," she says. "Lots of the connections in your brain—and in Elaine's—were stretched thin. They weren't broken. We caught it before the connections snapped. But they were damaged."

"I have brain damage," I say dully.

"Not necessarily," Jaylene says. "The brain is an amazing instrument. It regrows neural pathways, often on its own. Your brain had a lot of trauma, but its recovery is as startling as what we're seeing in the other cells in your body."

That explains the muzziness, though—why I feel like I'm thinking through clouds. Some of the pathways in my brain are blocked, shortened, thinner.

"I think if you had been in that field another ten minutes, you'd be dead," Jaylene says. "And if you'd been in it for another twenty, you probably would have ended up like those previous divers."

I shake my head, then wish I hadn't. "But I've gone into malfunctioning fields before."

"I know," Jaylene says. "Yash and I believe that what you and Elaine experienced is something else entirely. It's not a malfunction as we know it inside the Fleet."

"But Coop said, when he shut down the Room of Lost Souls—" then I pause, and use the Fleet name. "I mean, Starbase Kappa. When he shut down the *anacapa* there, that it was just a malfunctioning field."

"You operated for a long time in this particular field," she says. "You were having trouble, but I don't think it's what our instruments registered as the malfunction. I think you, and Elaine, and your mother if what Mikk tells me is true, were experiencing something that we're not measuring."

Her cheeks flush, then she shrugs prettily.

"But," she says, "that's really just a guess. It's going to take scientists to figure this out."

I rub my poor damaged forehead with the first three fingers of my right hand. I can't feel anything different in the skin or in my fingertips. But inside, there's still a sense of absence. I wonder if that's from the extreme pain, if the brain is still recovering. Or if it knows it lost something it might never recover.

"This isn't making sense to me," I say finally. "I don't know if that's because of the damage or—"

"Perhaps we should wait and see," Jaylene says.

I ignore that. I'm not quite communicating the way I want to.

"What I mean is," I say, "we brought people with the genetic marker into similar fields, and they were fine. *I* was fine until this one. I have the marker. So does Elaine. We've never had trouble before."

Jaylene nods. Her lips are thin. "I'm hoping that Yash and Mikk discover something. This is not my area of expertise. I'm not sure what's going on. I personally think it's a combination of factors. That field was stronger here, in the Boneyard. Whether the field was amplified by something else here or whether we encountered something new, I don't know. But there were differences that we knew about from the start."

"And now the field is gone," I say.

"At the moment," she says.

"Between you and me," I say, "what do you think of Yash's idea of sending someone else in to shut down the rogue *anacapa* drive?"

Jaylene looks at me balefully. "I think it's the stupidest thing I've ever heard."

17

THE PHRASES "STUPIDEST THING" and "shut down the drive" echo in my head for the next two days. We have no good choices, and I'm thinking about all of them.

We might end up choosing the option with the least degree of stupid, as my old friend Squishy would say. Sometimes great risks require a little bit of stupid.

We took a great risk coming in here, and now we might have to take another great risk to get out.

I spend most of those two days in bed. By the middle of the second day, I'm feeling well enough to want to walk around. The dizziness is gone, and the scans Jaylene shows me are better. The cells look like cells again, albeit different than they had before.

She tries to explain the difference to me, using terms that are familiar but used in a way I don't entirely comprehend.

I understand situational medicine. I can wrap a broken arm, help someone who is oxygen deprived, figure out what to do about severe lacerations. I don't know the details of human biology. It doesn't interest me as much as spaceships and derelicts and wrecks and mechanical things.

So I'm at a bit of a loss when it comes to the details of my own condition. I never expected to be in bed so long. I never expected to be so weak.

I figured, if something happened to me while diving, I would die out there. I never expected to be saved. I never expected to be damaged.

I never expected to be weak.

But I try not to dwell on it. I am improving, and rapidly, according to Jaylene. So is Elaine. We haven't had a chance to talk yet, because Jaylene believes we both need rest more than companionship.

She's right about the rest. I've fallen asleep in the middle of conversations. I'm still shaky at times.

I don't like how I feel.

I also don't like what I know.

I know I won't be diving in the next few days, or even the next few weeks. I know there's a possibility that I might never dive again.

But I don't discuss that either. I don't want people to tell me I'm being too pessimistic. I also don't want them to tell me that I'm right.

I'm dozing for the fifth time today when Yash and Mikk enter my room. They pull up chairs beside the bed. They look determined.

I square my shoulders, scrunch my pillow behind my back, and pretend to have more energy than I do.

I force myself to focus.

"Okay," Mikk says without preamble. "Here's what we know. Whatever that energy field was—and we'll discuss that in a minute—it came out of the runabout."

I look away from his face to Yash's. She nods.

"We checked every ship around the runabout again," Mikk says. "Then we used that program Yash's team was writing when you and I gave them all our information. Her program is very different from ours."

"It works this way," Yash starts, but I wave a hand.

"Tell me that later," I say. "My ability to concentrate still fades in and out. Let's make sure I'm completely focused for the important stuff."

She nods, but looks disappointed that she can't explain how brilliant her team was.

"Both programs found the same things," Mikk says. He and Yash clearly planned the tag team part of this little talk. "There are minor *anacapa* readings coming out of some of the Dignity Vessels nearby."

Yash winces at the word. Mikk clearly doesn't care about her feelings on that.

"Not all of those readings are of malfunctioning *anacapa* drives," he says. "Some are simply working drives that give off low-level readings."

That surprises me. Our search didn't turn up those *anacapa* drives, primarily because the signals they give off aren't what we used to think was stealth tech.

"The energy readings that trapped you and Elaine," Mikk says, "came out of that runabout. The readings were strong from the very start, but I hadn't realized how strong until after we brought the two of you back to the *Sove*, when I checked everything against our past data."

When he said "our," he meant his and mine.

Except for that moment when Yash started to tell me about her search parameters, she has sat quietly in her chair, watching both of us.

"You said the readings got stronger when I opened the runabout's door." I've been going over that and over that in my mind, wondering if I nearly got Elaine and I killed.

"The airlock door," Yash says. "The interior door."

"We're not sure if there was some kind of failsafe you triggered," Mikk says, "or if the energy was that much stronger inside the runabout."

"As far as I can tell," Yash says, "the runabout's hull isn't strong enough to contain that much energy. I'm guessing that something activated."

"Or it was coincidence," Mikk says. "Whatever was causing that energy was building, and we just happened to decide to dive the wreck right at the time the energy built up the highest."

They've clearly been having this discussion for some time. I can't tell if they want me to offer an opinion about it, or if they are simply going over a familiar argument, catching me up on it.

I decide not to have an opinion, not yet. I want to see the data. I want to come to my own conclusions.

But right now, the idea of reading all the data makes me even more exhausted.

"That energy field," Mikk says, "was not only stronger than anything we encountered in the past, but it's a little different."

He glances at Yash. I get a sense they're not telling me something.

"Different how?" I ask.

He shakes his head. "I can show you the information," he says, "but right now, we have no real interpretation for it."

"The thing is," Yash says, "the field is gone. It vanished shortly after we yanked you back into the *Sove* and it hasn't returned."

The word "yank" startles me, and makes it clear to me just how panicked they were as they were bringing Elaine and me back.

I had to get past my own reaction to what was happening to me. I can feel my concentration break.

I force it back to the conversation.

"You say that the field 'vanished,'" I say. "What does that mean, exactly?"

"It's as if the runabout doesn't have an *anacapa* drive at all," Yash says. "There's no reading from that little ship. None."

"And the *anacapa* reading hasn't returned?" I ask.

"Not at all. We're monitoring it constantly." Yash runs her hands over her knees, a nervous gesture I'm not used to seeing from her.

I frown. I know her hesitation about investigating further. I also know that she's worried we might not escape from the Boneyard.

I need to get myself healthy again. I don't have time to lie here any longer. I have to start moving.

I'm just not sure I can.

I scrunch the pillow up some more, and straighten my back, ignoring the growing exhaustion that makes my eyes want to close.

"Are the doors still open?" I ask.

Mikk looks at the door to my room here in the medical wing. After a second, Yash does too.

They don't understand me.

"In the runabout," I say. "Are the doors still open in the runabout?"

Mikk glances at Yash. She shrugs.

"We haven't looked," she says.

"You need to look," I say.

She nods. She understands immediately. But Mikk is frowning.

"Why?" he asks.

"Because one of your theories is that something blocked that signal," I say. "If the doors closed, then the signal might be less than it was, but still blocked from the outside. If the doors are open, then perhaps the signal has burned itself out."

Or something like that. There are a million theories as to why that signal would vanish.

But my idea might start Mikk and Yash on a new investigation.

"I hadn't even thought of that," Mikk says.

"I hope the doors didn't close," Yash says, one of her hands forming a fist. "If the doors did close, that runabout is still automated on some level. We got no indication of that either."

Mikk nods. Then he turns to me. "We have imagery from the interior of the runabout. We would like to look at it with you."

"You haven't looked at it yet?" I ask.

"Not the imagery," Mikk says. "We have combed the telemetry the probe has been sending us."

"That's another way we know there are no more readings," Yash says. "We got no energy signatures from the interior at all."

"And the probe is still inside," I say.

"Yes," she says. "Still sending us information."

"But I put it in there when that strange energy was at its peak," I say. "You need to send in a new probe."

Yash made her familiar *No way, that's stupid* face. She hadn't done that with me for quite a long time. I had almost missed it.

"Boss is right," Mikk says. He clearly caught Yash's expression as well. "The probe might not be inside the runabout we're looking at."

"What?" Yash turns toward him, visibly surprised.

"One of our theories about these malfunctioning *anacapa* drives," he says, "is that it creates some kind of temporal distortion. We might be looking at data from the future, not from the present."

I doubt that's the case. But I'm not sure how much of that is wishful thinking. I keep thinking about what Jaylene said, about the changes that happened on the cellular level occurring quickly rather than over days or weeks or months of perceived time.

I've also been thinking about that incredible crushing feeling in my head, the way that the music had nearly swamped everything about me. Maybe my mother's last few moments weren't spent contemplating beautiful lights and lovely music. Maybe she hadn't been thinking she had been abandoned by all who loved her.

Maybe she hadn't abandoned me at all.

Maybe she had been crushed completely within a few minutes of entering that room. Maybe we had been misreading this all along.

But I'm not going to say that, because all we do when faced with this strange energy is make suppositions about it.

We don't get actual data.

I'm proposing that Mikk and Yash try again, they get more data, and we actually learn something new.

"You think the probe is not even here?" Yash asks Mikk. "That it's in its own time field?"

He shrugs. "We have to explore all possibilities."

She looks at me, clearly just a bit annoyed.

"All right," Yash says, "but that doesn't change what we came to say to you. Do you want to look at the first visuals with us?"

Something in her face tells me she's less excited about the visuals now that she knows they might be from a different time frame.

But I'm not less excited. Because they might also be from now. And those images will tell us a lot about what's going on inside that runabout. Just seeing the layout alone will help.

"I do want to look at the images with you," I say, "but can it wait until tomorrow? I'm not sure I can concentrate much longer."

My traitorous eyes want to close again. I'm not sure how long I can keep them open—which irritates me beyond measure.

Yash's lips thin. She's clearly still operating on that make-believe timetable.

"Yes, we can wait," Mikk says. He was trained by me. The timetable is whatever we make it.

Yash frowns at him. I recognize that look of hers as well. She's about to argue with him.

He recognizes the look too. He shakes his head, just a little, clearly warning her off.

He's being protective of me. I've seen Mikk be protective of others on the team, but I've never seen him act that way with me. Which doesn't mean he hasn't been. I just haven't seen it before.

His gaze meets mine, and his cheeks flush just a little. He knows I've caught him defending me in a way that, had I been healthier, I might have objected to.

I don't say anything, which seems to concern him more. But I'm concerned. I'm not anywhere near full capacity, and it disturbs me.

"Waiting," he says in a tone that tells me he's talking to Yash more than me, "will allow us to send a second probe and get some telemetry back from it."

"If it can go inside the runabout," Yash says.

"Even if it can't," he says. "We'll get some readings from the exterior."

"I have to be clear about one thing." I sound tired even to me. The words are coming out slower. "No one is diving anywhere near that runabout until we know what's going on. Not even taking a line and going near the runabout like Elaine and I did. If we're sending a second probe, we do our best to get it inside the runabout from *inside* the *Sove*."

Mikk nods. "I was thinking the same thing. I should have said so."

"There's no way we would send anyone out into that—whatever it is," Yash sounds affronted that I even made the suggestion.

"You scared us, Boss," Mikk says so softly, I'm not sure he meant for Yash to hear it.

But she did, and she doesn't contradict him.

I should say, *Yeah, it scared me too*, but I decide against it. I've been preaching the dangers of diving for my entire career. I've seen a lot of injury and death, and while I've come close to serious problems throughout my diving career, I've never really had any of my own.

It was just my time, and I know that.

"It's a good reminder," I say, "that diving is one of the most danger-ous things we do."

To my surprise, Mikk grins. He reaches out, pats me on the hand, and says, "I knew you were in there somewhere. That's the first major sign that I've had that you're improving."

Yash isn't smiling. She looks from him to me and back again. Then she stands up.

"We will have the footage from the first probe tomorrow, no matter what," she says. "If we wait to view the information we get until after-noon, we might have information from the second as well."

"Then by all means," I say, "let's meet in the afternoon."

"But you tire easily," she says, sounding almost argumentative.

"I've heard of these things called 'naps,'" I say. "I might indulge in one."

Mikk's grin gets wider. Yash glares at me. Then she taps Mikk on the shoulder.

He stands too. He looks like he wants to say something more, but he doesn't. After a few platitudes directed at me, urging me to feel better, they both leave.

I slide back down on the bed, straighten out the pillows, and nearly fall asleep doing so.

I should feel more urgency about us being trapped in the Boneyard, but I don't. Some of that is the exhaustion I feel. I'm too tired to be scared, if that's possible.

But the bulk of it is something else. Underneath all the shakes and the fog and the tiredness, I'm intrigued.

It has been a while since I've faced a mystery ship.

I hadn't realized just how much I have missed them.

18

THE NEXT AFTERNOON TAKES FOREVER to arrive, partly because I'm feeling significantly better. I'm not one hundred percent. I feel like I've just come off one of the most difficult dives of my life, sweaty, exhausted, and wrung out.

But my brain is clear for the first time since I woke up, and I feel half-way human. In fact, I've had to fight most of the morning to keep myself in check. I want to walk around the medical wing of the ship, and maybe eat my way through everything I can find.

I don't, of course. Instead, I eat judiciously, and drink copiously, and let Jaylene poke and prod me to find out what, if anything, has changed.

When Mikk finally comes to get me, he seems surprised that I'm sitting in a side chair, dressed and ready. It's only in the reactions of others that I am slowly realizing just how close to death I might have been.

"Elaine will join us too," Mikk says. "I didn't clear it with you. I hope it's okay."

"She nearly died for this information as well. Of course it's okay," I say. "Is Yash getting her?"

"Jaylene will bring her. Elaine's not quite as mobile as you are." He looks a little strange. "She was injured in different ways than you were."

I flush just a little. I had asked if she survived, and I had also asked if she received the same treatment I had, but once I learned we had both awakened, I figured we were healing in the same way.

I always tell my divers to watch out for their assumptions. I had forgotten my own lessons.

Mikk stands near me as I climb out of the chair, not grabbing me and pulling me up, not touching me to help me stand, but close enough to catch me if I fall. Mikk isn't the kind of man who hovers, so the fact that he is actually shows just how worried he is about me.

We walk at my pace to one of the medical conference rooms. I had expected to go up three levels in the *Sove* to one of the regular conference rooms. Considering how ill I was yesterday, however, I understand this new change in venue.

The medical conference rooms on Dignity Vessels are smaller and much more comfortable than the conference rooms for crew. The medical conference rooms are designed for families to discuss treatments with doctors, rather than for the crew to make some kind of life-saving decision for the entire ship.

There is a central table, with screens that form over the surface, but the chairs are different. They're therapeutic chairs, designed for the ill or injured to sit in, and for the ill's doctors to set up the proper support. The chairs also diagnose, which chairs in the main conference areas do not. So, if I pass out here, Jaylene will know exactly why.

Or rather, if Elaine passes out. She's already here, propped up in one of the chairs off to the side, her legs extended before her, her arms resting on long armrests. A support holds her head in place.

She's so pale that she's almost translucent. Her eyes are sunken deep into her head. I've seen my own reflection today, and I don't look that bad. In fact, my skin has returned to an acceptable color. Not a "normal" color—I'm not there yet—but I look like someone who is tired, not someone who might die tomorrow.

I make my way over to her, and touch her arm. She tilts her head toward me, but doesn't turn. The right corner of her mouth is bent downward at an unnatural angle. She smiles, but the smile only reaches the left side of her face.

"Good to…see you," she says, her voice at a half whisper.

"You too," I say.

Jaylene sits beside her, almost protectively. Normally, I would object to a med tech sitting in on this briefing, but it's obvious that Elaine needs her. I don't feel like I need Jaylene, but had we had this meeting yesterday, I might have.

Yash sits at the head of the table, her entire body taut. She's watching both me and Elaine as if expecting us to die at any moment.

"Are we going to be able to do this?" Yash asks, and she's not addressing me or Elaine, but Jaylene.

Still, it's Elaine who answers. "I'll stay… as…as long as I can."

I wait half a second, contemplating how to respond. I don't want to say that I'm fine—because I'm not—but I'm so much better than Elaine. I know I can sit through an entire meeting and an entire discussion, and continue my improvements afterwards.

"Yes," I say. "We'll be able to do this."

Jaylene looks at me, but there's no assessment in the look like there had been in the days before. She isn't waiting for me to keel over or pass out. However, after her glance at me, she turns her attention to Elaine.

Clearly Jaylene is still worried about her.

Yash did not miss that small interaction. Her gaze seems to catch everything.

She takes a deep breath, and stands.

"All right," she says. "We sent the second probe inside the runabout this morning. The doors were still open."

I let out a small breath.

"Good," I say, about the probe, about the doors, about everything.

Yash glances at me, but doesn't do anything else to acknowledge me.

She says, "We have a lot of data that looks, superficially, like the data we got from the original probe. But Mikk and I and Zaria will go over it, just to make sure that we're not missing something. We'll be bringing in some of the trainees as well. I don't want to miss anything."

This time I don't respond aloud. It would seem odd for me to continually say "good," as if I'm encouraging her along.

I lean back in the therapeutic chair. It molds to my back, giving me support in ways that chairs normally do not. That feels odd, like someone is actually holding me in place.

"Mikk ran a program comparing the visual footage from both probes," Yash says. "With some slight differences, the visuals are exactly the same."

"Slight differences?" Elaine asks in that half whisper.

"We have footage of the second probe as it passes the first probe," Yash says. "Things like that."

Elaine tries to nod, but can't because of her neck brace. Or maybe her head is just wobbling. I don't know.

Looking at her makes me distinctly uneasy. I could have ended up just like that—and maybe I was when I wasn't conscious.

"So," Yash says, "we'll be using the footage from the first probe."

Then her gaze meets mine.

"And before you say anything," she adds, "we will do a visual comparison later, to make sure everything really is the same."

I hadn't been planning on saying anything, but clearly, Yash has me being critical of her in her head. Which is fine. It keeps her on her toes.

"Good," I say, because she expects me to.

"All right." Her hand hovers over the controls on the tabletop. "Just so you know, Mikk and I haven't really looked closely at the footage either. So we'll probably be as surprised as you are at some of the things here."

I nod. Elaine makes her strange little head movement.

Jaylene moves just a bit closer to Elaine, as if guarding her while we watch.

Yash brings her hand down, and the conference room dims. The screen behind her shows the footage from the probe.

Mikk and I learned long ago not to show footage from the probes in three dimensions. The probes don't have enough data to build the backs and sides of things, so everything looks a little compressed.

Instead, we watch in two dimensions, and sometimes see much more than we ever would in person.

I can tell right from the start that Mikk has edited a bit of the footage. The probe I had sent into the airlock was already active. Images of the probe going through the airlock were not there.

The footage starts inside the runabout itself. Nanobits float by like sediment. The interior of the runabout is falling apart just like the exterior.

No one had guided the probe, so it followed its programming. The programming was pretty elementary: examine everything swiftly at first and then up close.

So the moment the probe is inside the runabout, the images track through the small corridor.

Everything is canted slightly to the right. My brain adjusts instantly, which is a bit of a relief, considering how creaky it's been, but Elaine has to tilt her head slowly to the left to accommodate that difference.

Jaylene frowns at her, and so does Mikk. I don't like that much either.

But I focus on the runabout instead.

The design of the runabout is similar to designs I've seen from the runabouts on the *Ivoire*, but not quite the same. There are two crew cabins down the corridor. The cabins are exactly the same size, which is not how they had been designed for the *Ivoire*.

One of the cabins had a blanket floating near the right wall, a pillow trapped in a corner. God knows how long they've been there—it takes forever for items like that to decay in space, especially if they've been built to withstand the rigors of space travel.

The other cabin looks nearly empty, although it might not be if we can get inside.

I'm itching to dive this runabout now. I don't smile—I can't with Elaine so close—but I feel like me, the old me, completely, for the first time since I woke up.

The probe takes us back down the hall, navigating the floating nanobits like they're something that can actually harm the probe. It ducks into the galley kitchen, which seems oddly barren. Something's missing there, but I don't know what, exactly, because I'm not sure what's standard in an active Fleet kitchen.

The probe makes its way to the cockpit.

It looks like the cockpit/inflight area of one of the larger runabouts on the *Ivoire*. The runabout once had seats bolted to the floor behind the actual navigational equipment, but apparently two of the seats—at the very least—are gone. Only one passenger seat remains. It has gotten stuck in a reclining position.

Everything else seems intact. The pilot's chair faces the navigational equipment. And the screen across from the navigational equipment doesn't look damaged—at least as best I can tell using the grainy imagery from the probe.

I recognize the screen. It's like the screens on some of the smaller ships on the *Ivoire*, designed to show two-dimensional imagery or to open onto the space before it. Unlike most of the Fleet designs, some of these smaller ships do not keep their cockpits protected in the center of the ship itself.

If I am understanding the layout of this runabout, the cockpit wasn't protected here either. It was on the side of the exterior where Elaine and I ran into the most problems. I'll have to double-check this with Mikk and Yash, but it seems to me that's the case.

Like it was programmed to do, the probe spends time in the cockpit. It doesn't look at the standard seats or the pilot's chair, although I wish I could make it do so. Because there's something odd there.

The probe heads to the navigational equipment, which looks like it's intact. The navigational equipment doesn't appear to be working, which is not a surprise, but it doesn't seem damaged at all.

"I don't see an *anacapa* drive," Mikk says. "I've looked at this part of the footage, and I don't see anything."

"There are controls underneath the navigational board that I've never seen before," Yash says. "I suspect those are for the *anacapa*."

"But where's the drive?" Mikk asks. "It has to be in the ship somewhere."

The probe moves closest to the wall. Yash points at something just beside the panel, and on the floor itself.

"That's not quite big enough to house an *anacapa* drive that I'm familiar with," she says. "But the casing looks right."

"Would it be so close to the navigational controls?" I ask.

"I have no idea," she says. "But this is a pretty standard runabout layout, and there's nowhere else to put it that you can access it easily."

"How easily would you have to access it?" Jaylene asks, surprising me. I thought she was more focused on Elaine than the images floating by us.

"Quickly if something goes wrong," Yash says. "You can't hide it under the floors or in the ceiling."

"Did you see that hole in the corridor?" Mikk asks. "It looked like someone had dug in there for something."

I hadn't seen that. But the missing chairs didn't seem to be anywhere either, and that's odd.

"It looks like this might have been scavenged," I say, "but the navigational equipment looks untouched."

"Are scavengers…super…super…superstitious?" Elaine asks, her whisper cutting into our conversation.

We all look at her in the same movement. I guess none of us really expected her to contribute much to this meeting.

"Why?" Mikk asks.

"Because of…the corpse," she says.

"What?" Yash asks. She looks at Mikk as if she expects him to explain this.

He shrugs.

Elaine sees their surprise, and something in her face changes. She thinks they don't believe her because of her injuries.

"Can you pan?" she asks.

"We have what we have," Yash says.

"Then re…re…reverse," Elaine says. "I'll show you."

She struggles against the chair.

"I don't want you to stand," Jaylene says, but Elaine ignores her. Elaine rises, slowly, her head brace moving with her.

The chair changes shape, almost like it's reaching for her. She uses one arm of the chair to brace her left side. Her right side shuffles.

Jaylene and Mikk have stood as well, moving just close enough to Elaine to brace her if she falls. She looks determined not to.

She uses her chair, then another, and then another to stair-step herself to the edge of the table where Yash is. Yash takes a step closer to Elaine, but Elaine says, "Please move… back."

For a moment, Yash doesn't move at all. She doesn't seem to understand what Elaine wants, but I do.

"Yash," I say. "You're in her way."

"Oh," Yash says, and scrambles aside.

I get up as well, and Jaylene shoots me a glare that would have made me stop moving yesterday. But I'm all right. I'm healing, probably thanks to those nanobits.

Besides, if Elaine can move, I can too.

I walk down the other side of the table. Now Elaine and I are flanking Yash.

"What do you want me to reverse to?" I ask Elaine.

"I got it," Yash says.

I ignore her, keeping my hand on the controls. I have a hunch I know where Elaine is going with this.

"The first…gli…gla…when we first *see* the cockpit," Elaine says. Now I realize she's having trouble with words too. That must be very frustrating. "All the way to the… image of the navigation panel."

Yash reaches for the controls, but I have already mentally cued up those moments, so it only takes me a second to reach them. I had a hunch we were missing something.

Elaine stands near the footage, and as the probe's camera shows the gap between the chairs, it also focuses—just barely—on the pilot's chair. Something hangs down to one side, the side we couldn't see well. The side where Yash believes the *anacapa* controls are.

"Zoom…," Elaine says.

She doesn't need the next word. I know it. *In.* She wants me to zoom in on that hanging thing.

I do. It looks like the side of a hand.

Mikk curses slightly.

"Now," Elaine says to me. "Regular."

Yash is frowning, but I know what Elaine means. I return to the regular view that we'd seen before, moving just a little slower than usual.

"Where to?" I ask Elaine.

"Navigation panel," she says.

I move the image forward until we have a clear view of the navigation panel. What had looked like a shadow to me as we first viewed this wasn't.

It was another hand, resting on the navigation board.

I have no idea how that's possible, unless the hand is wearing a glove that will make it stick to the panel. The other hand is floating slightly—or it looks like it is—but the hand on the panel seems like it's resting there.

I don't want to think about how it remains attached without some kind of adhesive.

I zoom in on the hand. It's definitely a hand, and it's attached to an arm. Judging from what little bit we can see, it appears to be mummified.

Which means it has been in this runabout a very, very long time.

I look at Elaine. Her eyes are sunken even deeper into her face. But she smiles at me, and this time, it doesn't bother me that she can only move part of her mouth.

She's feeling triumphant, and I don't blame her. She saw something everyone else missed. I know how important that is after the last few days.

"Let's ignore the scavengers for a minute," I say to Mikk and Elaine.

Yash moves into my line of sight and crosses her arms, as if she doesn't want to hear what I'm going to say next.

But she does. She just doesn't realize it yet.

"This body looks mummified," I say, "and if it really is, and if it's somehow attached to that navigation panel, then it probably dates from whatever went wrong inside this runabout."

Yash is frowning at me. Mikk is nodding, though. And Elaine's smile remains.

Jaylene stands as close to Elaine as she can without letting Elaine know she's there. Right now, Elaine is balanced, and not noticing how badly she's been injured.

I'd like to keep it that way.

"That means the Fleet didn't store these ships," Yash says. "We take care of the bodies of our dead."

"Yes, you do," I say.

I had watched a Fleet funeral for the *Ivoire*'s first officer after he committed suicide. It was a sad and lovely affair, and clearly something everyone needed.

"But I wouldn't jump to that conclusion yet," I say.

Yash glares at me. "You can't tell me that we have become a heartless people over 5,000 years. That's not who—"

"That's not what I'm saying." I keep my voice low, and try to ignore the fact that Elaine has wobbled.

Jaylene doesn't ignore it, though. She grabs Elaine and helps her into the nearest chair. Elaine apologizes softly, and Jaylene, just as softly, says, "I'm impressed you stood that long."

Everything stops while that happens, but neither Yash nor I look at Elaine directly. We know she's feeling weak instead of proud of herself for managing this long, and we don't want to draw attention to how she's feeling.

"What I'm saying is this." I pause just a little for dramatic effect. "I'm saying that if the Boneyard is, indeed, run by the Fleet, as we suspect, then the Fleet doesn't look at these ships before scooping them up and moving them here. Nothing gets inspected at all."

"Why would anyone do that?" Mikk asks.

"This is some kind of first-stage round-up pen," I say. "Maybe the Fleet put it together so that derelict ships wouldn't litter the sector. Or maybe there's a system—"

"There usually is a system," Mikk mumbles. "The Fleet loves its systems."

Elaine half strangles back a cough. We all look at her. She makes the sound again, and I realize she's not coughing. She's laughing.

"Such an…understatement," she manages.

We all smile—Jaylene with relief more than amusement—and then I say to Mikk, "You're right. The Fleet loves its systems. And they're usually sensible."

"Usually?" Yash says softly.

I ignore that. "If this is a round-up pen, a place where they put the derelict ships they find until they have a purpose for them, then there's some way to sort them. And, I would assume, inspections come at that point."

"That makes sense," Mikk says.

"It explains the varied *anacapa* readings," Yash says. "They've been bothering me. If I were running this place, I'd make sure all the functioning *anacapa*s were shut off."

That surprises me. "What if you needed them?" I ask.

"What do you mean?" Yash asks.

I shrug. "I mean, what if you wanted to move one of these large ships out of the Boneyard and across the sector? The sector bases have *anacapa*s that can link with a ship's *anacapa*, right?"

"If they've found a signal, and feel it's necessary." Yash sounds a bit defensive and I don't blame her. The *Ivoire* ended up here because it had sent out a distress signal and rather than have that signal picked up by a sector base in their time period, the signal got picked up by an abandoned sector base in mine.

"The Fleet don't need to find these signals," I say. "If they put the ships in the Boneyard, they'll have a record of each."

"You'd think they'd shut down the malfunctioning *anacapa*s," Mikk says.

"You'd think," I say, "but that shield around the Boneyard will probably protect any ship outside of it, should there be a massive explosion."

"They'd lose everything inside here, then," Yash says.

"But if this is just a round-up pen of derelicts," I say, "it won't matter much. It's like having an explosion at a garbage dump."

The entire group is silent for a moment.

Then Elaine struggles a little, moving her head sideways. Jaylene steps closer to her, clearly worried.

"That…doesn't explain the… scavenging," Elaine says. She sounds exhausted—she probably *is* exhausted—but that's not stopping her from participating.

"You think it was done by the Fleet?" I ask.

"We wouldn't leave a body," Yash says, forcefully this time.

I agree with her, but I want to hear Elaine. I ignore Yash's comment by keeping my gaze on Elaine.

"We need to…see inside," Elaine says.

"You two aren't diving," Jaylene says to me and Elaine. "Not now, not again. Not on this trip. I need someone with real experience looking at you."

Elaine ignores her the way I ignored Yash. Elaine and I just stare at each other.

I think we both know we're not going to dive again this trip. But we both understand that only by being inside that runabout can we figure out even a little bit of what happened there.

"I don't like the mysteries," Yash says after a moment.

I let out a small laugh.

"I do," I say. "I really do."

19

WE HAVE TO END THE MEETING because we don't want to tire Elaine further. But if I'm being honest with myself, I'm tired too.

Not weary, though. Not discouraged. Rather excited in a way I haven't felt for years.

I let Mikk hover as he walks me back to my room in the medical wing.

"Would you do me a favor?" I ask.

"What's that?" He sounds a little wary.

"I'd like you to go over the data from my dive with Elaine one more time. Check our reports of the sounds getting stronger and compare them to the interior layout of that runabout."

He doesn't complain about the extra work. Instead, he says, "What are you looking for?"

"I'm relying on my memory and a strange sense of spatial relations," I say, "but I think that we had our worst experience near that casing which Yash believes houses the *anacapa* drive."

"You had your worst experience near the door," he says, "which is nowhere near the drive."

"Yes," I say, "things became desperate there. But we were having different sound experiences right from the start. I'm just curious about this."

"Why?" he asks. "We know what happened to you was caused by the drive."

He's right. But I think something might be there.

"Humor me," I say.

"All right," he says. "I will."

20

THAT NIGHT, I REMAIN AWAKE for a long time, going over everything in my mind.

Someone is dead inside that runabout. That someone mummified, just like my mother in the Room of Lost Souls.

But bodies that have been in space a very, very, very long time also mummify. It takes forever.

Still, the similarity to my mother bothers me.

I didn't ask Yash how that hand could adhere to the navigation panel. I'm not sure I want to think about it, but I know she has ideas.

I don't think the person in that ship is a scavenger, killed by the *anacapa* field. I don't know why I am of that opinion, but I am. Something strikes me as different here.

Both Yash and Mikk say that the *anacapa* field is now gone, but Yash wants to make sure the *anacapa* has burned itself out. I don't blame her. She's also afraid of activating the *Sove*'s *anacapa*.

I'm not sure how much of that fear comes from Yash's own personal experience of being stranded in foldspace only to emerge five thousand years in her own future.

I'm also not sure how much of a risk I want to take of that happening to me. I like to think of myself as resilient, but I'm not sure I want to prove it.

I also think Yash's fear that activating our *anacapa* drive as we try to leave might cause some kind of explosion is a good one, and one we probably should contemplate any time we come into the Boneyard in the future.

If, indeed, we believe that we have a future with the Boneyard. That's not a decision I want to make on my own. I want everyone who is running Lost Souls to consider it. We're closing a lot of doors if we abandon the Boneyard. We need to determine how much risk those doors are worth.

And then there's the other problems with causing an explosion as the *anacapa*s activate. We might end bringing all of that explosive energy back to Lost Souls.

Or we might end up lost in foldspace ourselves.

Which leaves only blasting our way out of the Boneyard, and again, that might hurt everything around us. It might also get the Boneyard to fire on us, and we have no idea what kind of weaponry is near us.

Yash and Mikk discussed this in depth together, but ultimately, I need to be part of the decision.

I have slept for days, and my healing at least is working.

But Elaine is still down.

After hours of thought, and being unable to sleep, I get up and make my way to Elaine's room.

There is no medical staff here because we're running such a limited crew. Jaylene is sleeping in the medical wing, but as hard as she's been working, she's probably out for the night.

I pad my way down the hall, being as quiet as I can. Despite the lack of sleep, I'm feeling energetic. Well, maybe not *energetic*, exactly. I'm not tired, and that feels really good.

Elaine's room is the only one with a closed door and a medical alert blinking to the side. If there were other medical personnel here, they could tap on that alert and see exactly what's wrong with the patient inside the room.

Unfortunately, she's on her own, as I was. I didn't mind. I hope she doesn't either.

I slip through the door. The room smells faintly of antiseptics and sweat.

Elaine lies in the middle of a large bed, curled on her side, blankets swirled around her as if she's been sleeping restlessly. There are three alert buttons near her, and another not too far from her left hand.

I stare at the alert for a moment, vaguely remembering that I had had that many as well. Someone had explained it to me, and I had forgotten until now.

I wonder how much of my life and memories from the past few days are just gone because of what happened. Then I set that thought aside. I'll worry about it later.

A chair sits close to the bed. It's not a diagnostic chair. It must be one of the chairs Jaylene has been using.

She hasn't been in my room as much these past two days. She's probably been here, worrying about Elaine.

I sit down.

"Elaine?" I say softly. If I can't wake her, I'll sit for a while. If she doesn't stir, then I'll leave when I get tired. "Elaine?"

Her eyes flutter open.

"Boss," she says in that half whisper. "Sh…should you be here?"

She's worried about my health. That touches me.

"Probably not," I say. "But I am. I want your opinion on something."

"My…?"

"Yes," I say. "You and I are the only ones on this vessel who've experienced that malfunctioning field. I think we're the only ones who are truly qualified to make an important decision."

She hasn't moved. She still remains curled in a semi-fetal position. But her eyes are alert.

"What decision is that?" she asks.

"Let me explain," I say.

It takes a while to review all the options, with their pros and cons. It also takes some time to explain the dangers as Yash perceives them, versus how I perceive them.

Elaine listens attentively, asking a few questions. Mostly, though, I can see her engagement through her eyes. She seems riveted and worried at the same time.

When I finish, she levers herself upright. It takes her a moment. Her right side is weak. I reach out to help her, but she glares at my hand as if it will hurt her.

I withdraw it, and let her take care of herself.

She leans on a pillow, visibly tired from the movement.

"We have no good choices," she says.

"I know," I say. "Apparently, we've had none since we entered the Boneyard."

She smiles at me. I'm getting used to the half smile. It might be the light, but it seems like she's gaining more mobility in her face.

I hope so.

"The problem is," she says, "you are not... involved."

I didn't expect her to say anything like that.

"What do you mean?" I ask.

"You have been...rescued," she says. "You are our...le...our...."

She looks visibly frustrated, as if the word eludes her. "You are our boss," she says.

"Yes." I don't know where she's going with this.

"If Orlando and I had been diving, not you, then what would you have done?"

"Exactly what Mikk did," I say. "I would have pulled you out."

"Yes," she says calmly. I love that calm. "Then what?"

I haven't thought about that. I frown, contemplating it, and as I think, I can almost see it.

"I would have immediately gone through the data, to see what happened," I say. "I would have reviewed everything, sent in a second probe immediately, and—"

"Dived...again?" she asks.

It would have just been me. Not Elaine, not Orlando. In Elaine's scenario, the two of them would have been hurt, not me.

"Yes," I say. "Of course."

She smiles. Because she's right.

I would have gone back, with whatever protection we could rig up, because I would need to get everyone out of here. I might have lost my life, and saved the entire team.

I would have had Yash talk me through whatever I needed to do to that rogue *anacapa* drive. Or I would have seen if I could move that runabout, and maybe blow it up farther away from the *Sove*.

I would have been taking action, not—I'm afraid—hovering over the people who were injured.

Yash is a woman of action as well, but she's used to a hierarchy, and when it comes to taking risks, she doesn't take them with people's lives. Her job is to take risks with equipment.

Coop, as captain, takes risks with people's lives. It's one of the things the two of us have bonded over. We know what it's like to lose people we're in charge of.

Yash has lost friends and colleagues as well, but never from an order she has given.

I reach over and touch Elaine's damaged arm. It trembles involuntarily, probably non-stop.

"Thank you," I say.

She nods, and I'm pleased to see it. Her head isn't wobbling as badly as it was. As she sees my expression, her face softens in sympathy.

"What will you do?" she asks, the words clear.

"I don't know," I say.

But I do.

And so does she.

21

THE NEXT MORNING, I discharge myself from the medical wing. Or I would have, if there were actual medical personnel in charge of me. Jaylene is a med tech, something I had forgotten as I was healing. She has no say over me, even if I were dying.

No one does.

Even though Yash and Mikk protest, I work with them as we go through the data. They think I'm still fragile, and they might be right. But I'm not paying attention to that.

We run simulations. We examine every single detail that we can find.

Mikk has already determined that my hunch was right: when Elaine and I felt the pressure from the energy field, we were near that casing. I'm not sure what that information tells us, except that if the *anacapa* is activated, it has a range. But I file that away, along with everything else.

The *anacapa* drive is strangely dormant at the moment. It shut itself off after we left, and it has not activated again.

Yash isn't sure what caused it to shut down, and is going with the theory that the drive burned itself out. But everything about that drive is different from what we know of *anacapa* drives.

It's smaller, it's in a runabout, and it caused injury to two of us with the genetic marker—injury that we haven't received in any malfunctioning *anacapa* field before.

I don't trust Yash's theories.

Nor can I listen to her fears.

In fact, I cannot react from fear. I need to protect my team, not hide with it.

We didn't just come here to dive a Dignity Vessel. We're also coming to the Boneyard for answers.

There are answers on that runabout. There are also more questions than Yash is comfortable with.

But we need to get information, and we need to go where the information will take us.

We have a window of quiet. No malfunctioning *anacapa* drive, and no more strange energy readings—that we can find, anyway.

We have an opportunity.

We need to take it.

22

"No way in hell," Mikk says. "We are not risking you."

Another day has gone by—another day wasted—and I am standing on the bridge of the *Sove* with Yash, Mikk, and Orlando. We've gone over even more footage from the two probes.

"You want me to risk other lives, but not my own?" I ask. "I'm back to one hundred percent."

I'm not back entirely to 100 percent—if I've ever been 100 percent—but I've felt worse when I've dived in the past. Much worse, in fact. I can do this dive *now*, if nothing changes.

The problem is that Elaine is still not better, and I'm not sure she will be, if we don't get her back to Lost Souls soon.

What I'm really worried about is that we might have missed the window to help her days ago.

"We don't know that you're back to one hundred percent," Yash says. "None of us has enough medical experience to know that."

"None of us—not even at Lost Souls—has the medical experience to know what happened to me," I say. "So we won't know what's going on, exactly."

"Yet another reason not to have you dive," Mikk says.

I take a deep breath, trying not to get too angry. If I get too angry, I'll alienate them further. This crew doesn't make its decisions by emotion; they're guided by logic, which is usually a good thing.

"All right," I say, and I hear the challenge in my voice, but I can't seem to make the challenge leave my tone entirely. "Who dives this, then? Because we have to. Believe it or not, it's the least risky proposition, given what we know."

"Lots of qualifiers there," Yash says.

"Yes, there are," I say. "Diving is risky. It's my job, as the person in charge of this dive, to examine and manage risk. Right now, that dive is the best thing we can do. A dive might cost us another diver. But it also might get all of us out of here alive, without damaging the *Sove*, the Boneyard, or any of the other ships we want to dive in the future. As a bonus, this dive might give us other information that we might need for our own research. Important information, not just on how ships work, but on what's happening with the Fleet, right now."

I want to add *If the Fleet still exists*, but I don't. I don't want to antagonize Yash further.

Yash's mouth sets in a thin line. She knows I added that last to manipulate her.

The thing is, it worked.

"All right," Yash says tightly, "if you think we need to do this, Orlando and I will dive."

Orlando doesn't say a word. In fact, he has moved back just slightly so that he has physically made it clear he's not part of this conversation. He's just listening.

He's a very smart man.

"You and Orlando," I say to Yash. That challenge is still in my voice. My tone would alienate *me* if I heard it. I'm trying to modulate, but it's not working well. "I initially thought of that pairing and ruled it out."

Yash shakes her head, but Mikk is the one who speaks.

"None of the rest of the team we brought is going to be good at this kind of dive," he says. "The Fleet people have a lot of experience in space, but they don't know how to dive wrecks."

"I know," I say. It's pretty clear he and Yash have had this discussion.

I look at her now. She raises her chin so that her gaze meets mine full-on.

"You don't have experience diving this kind of wreck either," I say to her.

"I need to go on this dive," she says. "I have to see that *anacapa*. No one here has the *anacapa* experience I do. There's the possibility we can't bring it back to the *Sove*. I'm the only one who can shut the *anacapa* off on site."

Finally, I calm down just a bit.

I take a deep breath so that I sound calm too.

"There's no *possibility* that we bring the *anacapa* back to the *Sove*," I say. "That *anacapa* malfunctioned. We're not bringing anything that dangerous on board this ship no matter how much we believe we can contain it or if we believe we can shut it off."

Yash looks away from me, two spots of color on her cheeks. I'm a little stunned she even thought bringing the *anacapa* back here was a possibility.

"If it's deactivated, it's safe," she says.

"I'd trust you on the *anacapa*s you're used to," I say, "but not on this one. It's a completely different kind. You even said that. It's too small to be like anything you've seen before. God knows what else is different inside that container."

She takes a deep breath but doesn't argue with me.

"So," I say to her, "you're right. You're on this mission no matter what. An inexperienced wreck diver whose focus will be on equipment, not on the dive itself."

Those spots of color on her cheek grow.

"Orlando can handle that by himself," I say as if he's not here.

He's looking down, so that he doesn't meet my gaze, clearly pretending not to be here. I don't blame him. He usually doesn't take part in these planning sessions. He's usually told what to do and when to do it. He's not used to seeing this particular kind of fight.

"He's one of our best divers," I say. "He's a quick thinker and he's handled all kinds of difficult dives, including something that wasn't a dive at all."

Everyone looks at me. I can't believe they've forgotten.

"He was on the team in the abandoned sector base when the *Ivoire* first arrived," I say. "That's valuable experience. He knows how to handle the unexpected. He's done it many times before."

"So, it's decided then," Mikk says. He's used to dealing with me in these kinds of discussions. Sometimes he can shut me down with a declaration like this.

Sometimes.

"It is decided," I say. "I'm diving this wreck."

Mikk lets out a sigh of exasperation. "That's not what I said."

"I know," I say. "But here's why. You all think I'm not up to the dive."

"Yes," Yash says forcefully as Mikk says, "Yeah."

Orlando isn't saying a word.

"So think it through," I say. "The two divers—Yash and Orlando—get in trouble *inside* the runabout. You can't just yank them back to the *Sove* like you did me and Elaine. There are too many corridors and doors. You'd have to bring the entire runabout back into the *Sove* to save them, and that would endanger everyone."

No one says anything. They're all looking at me, even Orlando.

I turn to Yash, because she hasn't gone on a truly catastrophic dive with me. Not even Mikk was on the worst one, the one where I encountered my first Dignity Vessel.

"Normally, on a dive like that," I say, "we let the divers get themselves out. It's too dangerous to go in after them. And that might be the case here."

Yash doesn't move. She's with the Fleet. They're trained in deciding whether or not an individual is worth rescuing, in considering what would happen to the team.

"However," I say, "we're stranded here if we don't deal with that *anacapa*, so leaving the team probably isn't an option. We're close to the runabout, and depending on the scenario, we might be able to send someone in to untangle you, Yash, and Orlando, from whatever has you hung up inside. The key would be to get you physically outside of the runabout so that you can be pulled back to the *Sove*."

They're staring at me. Yash's face is a mask. Mikk's lips have thinned.

I straighten my shoulders. "You're saying that I'm not one hundred percent, even though I say I am."

Mikk's eyes narrow.

"Okay," I say. "Let me give you that assumption. Let's say that I'm not at my peak condition. That I might not be able to dive at my usual abilities."

Mikk closes his eyes. He knows where I'm going with this.

"Do you really want a diver who is not at her usual capability to dive in as the *rescue* diver? The person who has to act fast and make sure everyone is all right? Shouldn't the person in reserve be the *best* person we have, just in case something does go horribly, horribly wrong?"

I look at all of them. Orlando has bowed his head so I can't see his reaction. Yash hasn't moved.

Mikk sighs. "I don't like it," he says.

"I don't either," I say. "But all the evidence we have is that the *anacapa* field is gone. If that's the case, and what we're seeing from the probes is accurate, then this dive should be easy."

"It won't be," he says.

"I know that, and I don't expect it to be," I say. "But the data we have implies that it will. The trip from the *Sove* to the runabout is short, the runabout is small, and it looks like the *anacapa* drive is fairly easy to access. We won't know that for certain until we get there, but that's what we're seeing."

He's shaking his head slowly, disagreeing without saying a word.

"Do you have any other ideas?" I ask. The challenge is back in my voice.

"No." Yash finally speaks. I turn toward her. Orlando raises his head.

Of course, she would disagree with me. She hasn't done this kind of diving—

"I don't have other ideas," she says, and it takes me a moment to realize that her firm *no* a moment earlier wasn't in response to my entire idea. It was in response to my single question.

She doesn't have other ideas.

Neither does Mikk, and Orlando has moved himself out of the discussion.

"We are down a diver," Yash says. "We can take someone completely inexperienced or Orlando and I go, hoping that nothing will go wrong."

"You can't hope for that," Mikk says.

"I agree," Yash says. "Our history inside the Boneyard, let alone our history with this runabout, suggests that something will go awry. Orlando will do very well no matter where we put him. But we're limited to him and Boss as our most experienced onsite divers, because of those *anacapa* fields."

"And because of Elaine," Mikk says softly.

Her presence hangs over this discussion.

"We never asked you directly," Yash says, looking at Orlando, "are you still willing to dive the Boneyard?"

My breath catches. Yash has moved into our way of doing things without even realizing it. In the Fleet, people didn't get a choice.

I always try to give my divers a choice.

Orlando raises his head. He looks calmer than I expected, given how hard he's fought not to be in this conversation.

"Boss already asked me," he says quietly.

And that's all he says. We had a bit of a discussion the day before, mostly me reminding him of the risks and him listening as if I were insulting him ever so slightly just by bringing it all up and questioning whether or not he wanted to participate.

"What do you think about the dive?" Yash asks him.

"I think Boss and I should dive it," he says. "You can talk us through whatever we need with the *anacapa* drive."

"No," Yash says, before we even get a chance to discuss it. "I need to see that drive before I tell you how to mess with it. If I tell you to do the wrong thing, you *will* die."

Orlando's gaze meets mine. I suddenly realize that he thinks we'll die no matter what is going to happen. I'm not entirely sure that bothers him.

Most of us who dive feel it would be better to go out in the middle of a dive than alone in a bed like Elaine is right now.

"We're doing it my way," I say. "I'm going on this dive. Yash is going. Orlando will remain in the bay, waiting to come get us if need be. Mikk will run the dive from here."

"I don't like it," Mikk says again.

"I know," I say, and leave it at that.

23

I'M NOT SCARED.

Not as we map the dive using the interiors we pulled from the runabout. Not as we decide how we're going to keep verbally pinging the *Sove*. Not as we figure out how many tethers we're going to wear.

Not as we pull the equipment, and make sure it functions.

Not even as Yash asks the occasional stupid question, all of which I answer with great patience, at least according to Mikk.

I should be scared. I nearly died last time. Elaine might be permanently injured because of that dive. I nearly stepped off into oblivion like my mother had.

I should be terrified.

But I'm not.

It's as if I've seen the abyss, and while it's a painful place to cross into, I can face it now. I might not be able to handle it on a day-to-day level, but I know what I'm getting into.

If I die on this dive, I know how I will die. I know how painful it will be. I know how fast it will be.

And I'm ready for that. Just like I'm ready for the dive itself.

We are standing inside the bay where we had launched our last, horrid dive. Yash and I are suited up. Orlando is as well, because we all expect the dive to go badly.

He will remain here, with the bay door open, monitoring us. All three of us have tested our diving suits to make sure they function properly. I test and double-test mine, since I'm wearing my backup suit.

We all decided that the suit I wore on the last dive would be too risky to wear again.

This suit fits just the same as my usual suit, but it feels different against my skin. Newer, fresher, with just a little less give in the fabric. The oxygen smells fresher too, which tells me the rebreather in the other suit probably needed a better cleaning than I had originally given it.

Mikk is monitoring from the cockpit, along with some of the newer techs. He's training them, which we should have done earlier.

Elaine is there too. She wants to watch the dive. Mikk doesn't want her there, but I do. She's the only other person who knows how this particular malfunctioning *anacapa* field feels, and she's the only one who knows just how fast everything can crash in on you.

She's perfect. If she had just a little more energy, I would have considered having her run the dive instead of Mikk.

As it is, I made him promise he would listen to everything she said. He seemed a little affronted that I would be so firm about that, but I don't care.

Elaine is as valuable to this dive as Mikk is.

Orlando and I have just launched and secured the line between the *Sove* and the runabout. Yash is double-checking her tether. We decided we're only going to wear one around our waists so that we won't get tangled up in each other's tethers.

Mikk, who is clearly terrified of this dive, wants us to wear two.

Orlando has strapped his on as well, mostly to show Yash exactly how it's done. He double-secures hers. I don't think she notices, but I do.

And I approve. I don't want her to accidentally untether herself in the middle of a crisis.

Yash seems nervous. She made sure we're wearing gloves that enable us to tag things as dangerous. We made the tags shortly after we started diving the Boneyard months ago. She had worried that we might send ships back to Lost Souls without someone to adequately explain the dangers of what we find. So we have notifiers attached to our gloves.

Everyone back at Lost Souls knows to avoid the things marked "dangerous" until we can explain what we know about them or what they do.

On this dive, Yash and I will have to toggle back and forth between the notifiers and the markers for the handholds. Usually I just use the gloves to mark the best handholds for people who follow me.

But given the problems we've already had with this runabout, I'm happy to tag parts of it as dangerous.

"Hey, Boss," Mikk says in my ear, "are you sure you're diving today?"

I brace myself for a fight. Why is he bringing this up now?

"What's the problem, Mikk?" I ask, my tone cold.

"Your heart rate is normal," he says.

I let that information sink in for a moment. I'm about to dive and my heart rate hasn't gone up. I check in with myself. I don't feel overly excited. I'm happy to be diving, but that's a completely different emotion than the gids.

Orlando and Yash have heard him, but they don't say anything.

I do. I give them the chance I used to give my divers back when I ran my own wreck-diving company.

"Last chance to back out," I say to the two of them.

"If I do, what will you do?" Yash asks, her voice a bit clipped.

I shrug. "You and I will figure out how to handle the *anacapa*, with you here on the ship."

"I already told you that's not an option," she says.

I look at Orlando. His face seems filmy inside the hood.

"I'd love to join you," he says. And I can hear strength in his voice. Unlike Yash, he's not afraid of what's out there.

I wish he were diving with me.

"Well, next time," I say. "I hope I don't see you out there today."

"Me, too," he says, his tone serious. He pauses, then adds, "You ready?"

I double-check my tether, then tug on Yash's just to make sure. Then I nod at Orlando.

He's the one who is going to shut off the environmental controls inside the bay. Before he does so, we grab the handholds beside the bay door. Then he slams a palm on the control pad, and the environmental system shuts off. All three of us float upwards. I breathe normally inside my suit, and run the usual checks.

Mikk reminds Yash to do so through the comm. She nods quickly, apparently startled that she had forgotten something that basic.

I am forgiving. I'm usually the one who's a little off at the beginning of a dive, but I'm not this time.

I'm ready to go back out there.

"All right," Mikk says. "Unless there are objections, we're opening the bay door from up here."

"No objections," Orlando says. He's in charge of that door, of everything in the bay, really, including me and Yash. Again, that's how we designed the dive.

The door slides open, revealing the Boneyard. It always takes my breath away. Those ships, looking frozen against the blackness of space. The light filtering in from distant stars and just from the Boneyard itself.

And the faint hint of music, just like I always hear.

I half expected that music to upset me, but it doesn't. It's familiar and comforting.

"I'm going out first," I remind Yash.

Since she forgot to do her double-check, I'm going to assume that she's going to forget things until we get inside that runabout's cockpit.

"You'll have to tell me if I'm going too fast," I say to her.

"I will." She sounds nervous. I'm not used to that. Yash usually covers her emotions well.

I ease myself down, keeping my left hand on the handhold and with my right, I grab the line we've tethered to the runabout.

Then I step into the Boneyard.

24

THE MUSIC IS SO FAINT it sounds like someone is playing their favorite tunes loudly on a different floor of the ship. The sound is there, but not any more noticeable than the light filtering around us.

I check the line to make sure it's actually hooked to the runabout. I've gone on dives where the line wasn't hooked up properly, and fell away as we started to use it as a guide.

This line remains taut. I sink beside it, enjoying the sense of weightlessness. I pull myself along, focusing on that runabout.

The runabout's doors are still open, as I left them. Nothing else looks different, even though the data stream we got was right: I'm not hearing that choral music at all. The music that was so distracting on my first dive toward the runabout is completely gone.

The line bobs in my hand as Yash joins me. I stop moving and turn just enough so that I can see her. I can't see her face because I'm too far away. The light and ships are reflected in her faceplate, blocking my view of her.

She waves at me with her right hand. I like the touch of whimsy.

"I'm not hearing anything," she says, sounding tense.

"Your comm is off?" I ask, suddenly worried.

"No," she says, proving that the comm works just by responding to me. "I'm not hearing that music you and Elaine heard."

"I barely hear it," I say. "It's nothing like it was that day."

"Good," Yash says in a near whisper. "Really good."

I agree. We aren't quite in the clear, but things aren't as bad as they were that day.

We're running a time check on this mission, but we don't have a time limit. We never even discussed one, because we all want to get this done. I'm hoping for a quick in and out, although I don't say that.

I don't want to hurry Yash.

Still, we make it to the runabout in what seems like record time. I check my time with Mikk, and we are clocking everything exactly to the second, which is good. If I remember correctly, we were already a thousandth of a second off the last time we reached this point.

I make myself focus on this dive. We will go in, check the *anacapa*, and get out. That's all.

I reach the side of the runabout, and cling to the exterior door. The nanobits float around me, disturbed by my presence, but I don't hear any music at all here. That seems strange to me, but I don't comment on it.

Instead, I turn slightly, and watch Yash make her way across the line, one rather nervous handhold at a time.

She reaches my side much more slowly than I would have liked. Part of me still wants Orlando on this dive. He and I would have been inside already. We would have made our way to the cockpit, and maybe even to the drive, depending on what we would have discovered.

I hadn't thought this through, working with a newer diver. I hadn't realized how slowly we would have to go.

Still, I make myself smile at her in case she can see into my hood. Even if she can't, she can hear the smile in my voice.

"Ready?" I ask her.

She takes an audible breath. My suit might not be recording any gids from me, but I'll bet hers verges on gids for her.

"Honestly," she says, sounding a little surprised, "I can't wait to see this."

I hadn't expected the enthusiasm from her. I think I expected more fear. My smile becomes a real one.

I grab the edge of the outer door, and slide into the airlock.

I don't remember the interior of the airlock much at all. I just remember that interior door. It shows up in my dreams, only without the handprint in the center of it.

That handprint is mine.

I touch it, like a talisman, remembering slapping my palm against that door trying to get it to open. It's open just far enough now for me to slip through uncomfortably.

I think Yash can get through that opening as well.

More nanobits float around me. This runabout is sloughing off materials at a surprising rate. Or maybe we just disturbed so many of them that have fallen off over the years.

Yash pulls herself into the airlock as well. It's bigger than I realized. Both of us can float in here comfortably. I suspect Orlando and Mikk would fit in here as well.

This runabout is well designed, like all Fleet ships. Most small ships of Empire build don't have spacious airlocks, apparently not considering what might happen if a group of people needed to get inside quickly.

Yash looks at the walls, then runs a gloved finger over one side, releasing more nanobits.

"This thing is falling apart," she says.

"Yeah," I say.

"Have you marked it already?" she asks, and I know she's not referring to simple handhold marks. She means *danger* marks.

"No," I say. I wasn't planning on marking the runabout itself, but that makes sense given the problems we have.

She reaches up, places her glove on the center of the airlock door, and runs her thumb along the edge of her forefinger, where the mark trigger is.

She moves her hand away. The *danger* sign flares blue. Beneath the word *danger*, which is written in both the Fleet's Standard and modern Standard, is the name of the Lost Souls Corporation. She actually added a "property of" tag, which I hadn't expected.

It was a brilliant thing to do, in case this runabout ends up somewhere unexpected—which, given everything else that's happened, wouldn't surprise me.

I nod toward the small opening in the interior door. "Can you fit through that?"

I know she can, but that matters less than what she believes. If she struggles to squeeze through, she might damage her suit.

"Yes," she says.

"Time check," Mikk says.

Both of us give him the time on our clocks. Again, we're not finding a difference. That bothers me. I'm not sure why this dive would be so dramatically different from that first one.

My muscles tense. I let out a long breath, reminding myself to relax.

I check my own vitals, though, and nothing is unusually elevated.

The nerves haven't even reached my usual diving levels.

"Okay," I say to Yash. "Then let's go inside."

25

I SLIP IN FIRST, of course, marking handholds for Yash. She's good at some parts of diving, but not others, and I worry that she'll touch the wrong thing or activate something she shouldn't have.

I want us both to get out of this alive.

I grab a built-in handhold in the corridor, designed for anyone inside the runabout to grab if the artificial gravity fails. I hold myself in position, waiting for Yash to squeeze through.

I'm thinner than she is, and so had no trouble making it through that opening. I've been in tighter spaces.

But she's never done this—at least, not with me—and I want to make sure she's fine.

She slides through as easily as I did. She reaches up for my handhold, and we hang there together for a moment, getting our bearings.

The interior looks bigger than it had on the video from the probe. I've had that happen before; imagery changes your sense of things. I don't move yet because I want us both to get used to the real interior rather than the one we imagined.

The nanobits float here, making the interior seem murkier than it is. I reach up and flip on my headlamps, as well as the lights in my gloves. I don't use all of the lights on my suit, though. That would blind Yash, and probably make this entire trip useless.

I've already told her that we're not going into the crew cabins or the kitchen. Much as we could learn from those spaces, our only mission on this trip is the *anacapa* drive.

Yash believes that if she shuts off the drive, we might be able to bring the runabout home in the *Sove*. I haven't yet told her that the runabout is never getting any closer than this to the *Sove*. Maybe we'll ship the runabout home in a Dignity Vessel down the road, but it certainly won't be in a vessel with an unprotected crew on board.

Yash and I both turn our heads toward the cockpit at the same time. It's as if we both have the same thought: *we're settled in this runabout. Now it's time to move forward.*

So we do.

I lead, pulling myself toward the cockpit door. I hear nothing except my own breathing, steady and even. It feels a little odd not to hear anything. I keep expecting some tiny thread of music, like I usually hear in the Boneyard, but there's nothing.

The galley kitchen seems dark and foreboding on my left, although I can't say why I find it ominous. I ignore it as I pass, but stop before going into the cockpit. I grip the door frame, and look back at Yash.

She's peering into the kitchen.

"Something in there we need to look at?" I ask.

"It looks like someone tore it apart," she says. "Who would do that?"

"Scavengers?" I say.

"Yes, but it doesn't look like anything's missing." Then she shakes her head slightly. "That I can see anyway."

She pulls herself toward me. I wait until she's by my side again, before we ease ourselves into the cockpit.

Like the airlock, the cockpit is larger than I expected. It looks like four large seats had been locked into place when this thing left wherever it left from, with clamp-down bolts for more. Parts of the missing seats remain bolted into the floor. The reclining seat looks oddly comfortable. It's certainly big enough for someone as large as Coop to rest in comfortably, but it can clearly be modified for someone with a much smaller frame.

This little runabout had originally been built for a small group to travel in comfort to wherever it was going. And with an *anacapa* drive, they could easily have gone anywhere.

Yash immediately pulls herself toward the navigation panel. She stops before she reaches it, her hand clinging to the pilot's seat.

It bobs slightly.

I move toward her.

"She's strapped in," Yash says, "and she used something to hold her hands in place. Why would someone do that?"

"The gravity gave out?" I ask.

Yash shakes her head again. "I don't know," she says. "I've never seen anything like it."

I pull closer, then grip the navigation panel so that I can look at the corpse.

It's clearly female, but it's not wearing a uniform. I have no idea if she had been wearing one when she got stranded wherever she got stranded, if she got stranded at all. She might have died in a battle or something, which would also explain attaching the hands to the controls, so that she could work in a zero-g environment.

She has mummified, and wisps of hair—maybe brown, maybe black—float around her face. Her mouth is open, but I'm not sure if that means anything.

"What do you think happened to her?" Yash asks.

"I don't know," I say. "We'll have time to speculate later. Right now, we need to finish this mission."

Yash nods, then joins me at the navigation panel, which surprises me. I expected her to go for the *anacapa* drive immediately.

"You going to try to start this up?" I ask.

"No," she says. "I wanted to look at those controls I'd never seen before I tried anything with the *anacapa*."

I almost say that she's probably never seen anything like this runabout, considering it's much newer than the *Ivoire*, but I don't. I let her hover over the navigational controls, poking and prodding at things I don't entirely understand.

For a moment, it lights up, and she almost lets go in surprise.

"Huh," she says. "Who knew this thing had power?"

Then the lights fade, and the navigational panel is as dark as it was when we arrived.

Neither of us say anything more. She places a piece of equipment she had strapped to her belt on the navigational panel.

"What's that?" I ask.

"In theory, it'll pull data off the panel," she says. "I thought using it was a long shot, but considering that the panel just activated, this might not be as long a shot as I thought."

She peers underneath the panel at those controls.

"The controls detach," she says, and reaches upwards.

I put a hand on her shoulder. "*Anacapa* first," I say.

"Unhook that," she says to me, waving a hand at those controls. "They look like something we might be able to use."

"With the *anacapa*?" I ask.

"No," she says. "In developing our own equipment."

"Yash, if it's what caused the *anacapa* to go wonky—"

"It's not," she says. "Trust me. The *anacapa* went 'wonky' on its own. These are something else entirely."

I have to trust her on this, because even after years of working with Fleet equipment, I know very little about all its permutations.

"You see," she says, pointing at the edge of the extra panel, "it attaches here. You won't hurt anything if you detach it."

"With what?" I ask.

"Whatever works," she says.

At that moment, Mikk speaks in my ear. "You're twenty minutes into this dive. You have one hundred and twenty minutes of oxygen. Pay attention."

"I am," Yash and I say in unison.

I do a time check with Mikk. We're still exactly on the same time, which is also unusual in the Boneyard.

"I can see you now," he says.

"Huh?" I ask.

"The probes," he says. "They're still sending."

We hadn't been certain they would be. We speculated that they might have reset themselves to a loop.

I look around the cockpit, and finally see one of the probes, wedged into a far corner. I can't see the second probe.

Yash has worked her way around the pilot's chair rather than disturb the corpse.

"You know," she says as she finishes her trip to the *anacapa* container, "we should probably have some kind of service for her."

It takes me a moment to realize she's talking about the corpse.

"I don't feel right setting her adrift inside the Boneyard," I say.

"I don't feel right leaving her here," Yash says. "She clearly wanted out of this place. She wouldn't have lashed herself to the controls otherwise."

I can think of countless reasons why she had done that, but I don't say any of them.

Yash and I have a job to do, and we need to focus on that.

"What's going on with the *anacapa*?" I ask.

"The container's closed," Yash says. "I'm marking it dangerous, and then I'll open it."

While I appreciate her caution, I'm feeling a new sense of urgency. Mikk roused it in me when he reminded me of the time.

Even though this isn't a timed dive, we do have limited air. We have to pay attention, and not push any limits.

I position myself underneath the navigation panel and look at the controls that have Yash so intrigued. They are a separate piece of equipment, which surprises me. Usually, the Fleet doesn't pile pieces of equipment on top of each other. I can't tell if this is jury-rigged or if it was put here by a Fleet engineer.

In spite of myself, I'm intrigued now too.

The equipment seems to be attached with some kind of adhesive, not with bolts. I keep one hand on top of the panel, careful to stay away from the area most likely to have actual controls, and use the other hand to gently tug at the panel.

It doesn't move.

I position my headlamps so that I can see if there's space between the bottom panel and the top panel.

"Got it," Yash says. "The *anacapa* container's open."

My heart starts pounding. I don't hear any music, which is a good thing, but I'm not sure what we're going to find.

As if hearing my uncertain thoughts, Yash adds a single syllable of her own.

"Huh," she says.

"What?" I ask, trying not to sound as on edge as I feel.

"This thing looks normal," she says. "Smaller than I'm used to, but it's a standard *anacapa* drive. It doesn't look decayed or damaged. I'm not sure why it was malfunctioning. Or if it was malfunctioning."

"You heard the sounds," I say. "You measured the field."

"Maybe our equipment was off," she says.

"I don't think so," I say. "We got our strongest measurements on the energy field on the runabout's exterior outside that spot where you are right now."

"I know," Yash says, sounding annoyed. "But I don't see any explanation for this. I'd like to take it with us."

"No," I say as firmly as I can. That *anacapa* drive isn't getting near the *Sove*. "Get what information you need to off of it, and then we leave."

She sighs audibly, like a child denied a toy.

"All right," she says.

I return my attention to the control panel. There's a thin ray of light between it and the navigation panel. I can probably sever it with my knife, if I'm very, very careful.

I unsheathe the knife. I'm always exceedingly careful with it. One mistake, and I've sliced open my suit.

I keep the blade as far from me as possible. I slide it between the control panel and the navigation panel, only cutting at what I can see. I don't want to sever wires—not that the Fleet usually uses wires—and I don't want to interfere with any major fields of any kind.

Half the panel detaches. It doesn't drop, of course, but given time, it might just slide away.

I sheath the knife, then grab the edges of that control panel. I tug gently with one hand, making sure the other hand stays braced.

The panel comes off.

"I got the control panel," I say to Yash.

She rises up like a ghost on the far side of the corpse. Yash is indistinct because of all of the nanobits floating around us.

"Great!" she says, sounding more enthusiastic than I've ever heard her. "How much more time do we have in here?"

"Not much." The answer doesn't come from me. It comes from Mikk. But I concur.

We're pressing our luck in here.

"Okay," she says. "Just let me close this container and—*shit!*"

I pull myself up higher, still clutching the control panel.

Yash's entire suit is bathed in a gold light. She looks like she's being flooded by spotlights.

"What the hell?" I say.

She sounds oddly calm as she answers me. "This *anacapa* just activated," she says.

26

I TURN TO YASH. She's still bathed in that gold light, her face focused downward at that *anacapa* drive.

"What did you do?" I ask.

"It doesn't matter what I did," she says. "It's *active*. We have to get out of here. *Now*."

She grabs the navigation panel, cursing the whole way. I have no idea how long it takes an *anacapa* that's been completely deactivated to activate, but judging by Yash's reaction, it doesn't take much time at all.

"Orlando can't tug us out of here," I say. "We have to get to the doors."

"I know," Yash says, pulling herself over the navigation panel. She bumps the corpse, mutters, "Sorry," and then grabs that small device she had placed on top of the panel.

She can't keep moving this slowly, and I only have one free hand.

"I'm dumping this control thing you had me get," I say, and she doesn't argue.

I let go of the control thing and snatch her arm, pulling her forward, using my other hand to grab the handholds we had used before. I'm yanking us out of the cockpit as quickly as I can.

As we reach the doors to the cockpit, she stops being deadweight. She grabs and pulls too, and we're propelling along, moving as fast I would move on my own.

Behind us, lights switch on.

"Oh, shit," I say.

The last thing we need is for the full environmental system to engage. Full gravity will slow us down, not help us.

"I thought this runabout was dead," I say.

"I thought it was too," Yash says.

"Then how is this happening?"

"I have no idea," she says.

The lights reflect off the gray nanobits, nearly blinding me. I shut off my headlamps as I move forward, praying that the doors stay open.

"What's going on?" Mikk asks. "We're getting energy spikes."

"Tell Orlando to get ready to drag us out of here," I say. "The moment he sees us at the exterior doors, we will need help."

I can't believe I'm asking for help a second time while inside this damn runabout.

Yash is now side by side with me, propelling us forward along with me. We're working hand over hand—my hand, her hand, my hand, her hand—as we go.

Then she curses again, something nasty and guttural in her own tongue. Half a second after she finishes the word, I see what's caught her.

The airlock door has closed.

"Dammit," I say.

"What?" Mikk asks.

Normally, I would tell him to shut up and let us concentrate, but I like his voice in my comm right now. That means the *anacapa* hasn't fully activated. We haven't left here yet.

"Let me," Yash says, and rips her arm out of my grip. She moves forward at a faster pace than I knew she was capable of, and she heads to that airlock door.

She's moving so fast, she almost slams into it. Then she spreads her gloves against it. Nothing happens.

She taps in a code, and still nothing happens.

I reach for my lever. If nothing else, we're prying that damn door open.

Then she does something else with the controls, rapidly, something I can't really see, given the nanobits and the weird lighting, and the position of her body.

The airlock door doesn't open partially. It opens all the way.

"Hurry!" she says to me.

I don't need to be told twice. I follow her into the airlock, and the interior door closes behind us.

But the exterior door doesn't open.

"It's on a timer," she says, and I know she's right. The runabout probably has a program to let out the old environment and allow the people in the airlock to adjust to the pressure of the space they're about to go into.

"We don't have time to wait for that," I say.

"I know," she says, reaching for another control panel.

Then the exterior door opens just a little. Something has wedged itself between the door and the frame.

"Wonderful," Yash says. She's closer to that part of the door than I am. She braces her feet on the wall, grabs the door and shoves it toward the other side of the frame.

I brace myself and shove as well.

The exterior door opens a little farther and she squeezes out. Then a hand reaches in for me.

It's not her hand. It's too big.

I grab the hand, and let it pull me out of the runabout. The person holding me is Orlando.

He shoves Yash toward the *Sove*, then turns to me. "We have to unhitch," he says.

He's right. No one's in the *Sove's* bay, so the line hooking the *Sove* to the runabout can't be removed. Mikk will have to come down from the bridge to disconnect us.

I doubt there's time for that.

As I think it, the door slams shut, letting off a wave of nanobits. Orlando has grabbed the edge of the line, and is decoupling it.

I help him.

The line comes free, and he drops it. He's wearing a tether, just like I am.

We look at each other, like kids playing free-fall games in one-eighth gravity, and then shove off the side of the runabout. We tumble backwards, away from the runabout, careening in different directions.

I don't care if we make it to the *Sove* right away. We just need to be as far from that runabout as possible.

I don't want to think about the waves of energy that will come at us as the runabout's *anacapa* fully activates, nor do I want to think about what might happen if the runabout vanishes into foldspace while we're still out here.

I'm not quite enjoying the tumble, that free-spinning moment when I'm head over feet over head over feet over head, but I'm not hating it either. Around me I see ships, everywhere, bits and pieces of ships, then the two looming Dignity Vessels—the *Sove* and the new one, the one we initially meant to dive.

I don't see Orlando or Yash. It almost feels like I'm alone out here, spinning in the Boneyard, but I know I'm not.

And I have to stop this spinning or I will hit something.

In the middle of my spin, I reach for the tether. Not on my belt, because I don't want to accidentally dislodge it, but as far away from the belt as my arm can reach.

I pull on the tether as if I'm trying to clear up some slack rope, and for a few minutes, I worry that I might be tangled in the tether in a very dangerous way.

Then the tether gains some tension. I leave parts of it behind, and use it to "climb" hand over hand toward the *Sove*.

I've stopped spinning, but my head continues to feel like it is. My eyes haven't really focused. My entire system's equilibrium is screwed up, one of the many dangers of spinning free-fall.

I make myself focus on the side of the *Sove*, the open bay door, the floating unattached line. That's what my eye can hold the best—that unattached line. I watch it work its way toward the *Sove* as I do as well.

I don't see Orlando or Yash. Just that line, wrapping up, and that black opening where the bay door is.

Then I hear a gasp in my comm.

"Boss!" a voice says, and I don't know whose it is. It's female, but not Yash, and it sounds terrified.

I ignore the fear I'm hearing, and I keep pulling myself toward the bay door. I'm moving faster than I was, and I finally realize that someone—something—is pulling me inside.

I reach the lip of the bay door, and hands reach down, dragging me inside. They fling me in, and I spin again in the empty bay, moving so fast I nearly hit the wall on the far side.

Lights come up, and gravity returns, and rather than rebounding off that wall, I land on the bay floor so hard that it knocks the wind out of me.

My suit goes all kinds of crazy because I'm not breathing.

I'm dizzy, my eyes are watering from the pain of having all the breath slammed out of my body, and gravity feels like a heavy blanket forcing me downward.

Hands grab at my hood, detaching it, pulling it off.

I'm looking at Orlando, his face red, his hair glistening with sweat.

"Yash?" I manage, afraid of the answer.

"You can't get rid of me that easily," she says.

I sit up—or try to. I'm so dizzy I might throw up. I lay back down. The bay is spinning, and I can't seem to make it stop.

"It's gone." Mikk's voice is big and booming inside the bay. He's not using the comms. He's speaking through the ship's intercom system, for everyone to hear.

"What is?" Orlando asks, but he really doesn't have to. I know what Mikk meant.

The runabout is gone.

If we had been any slower, we would have disappeared with it—God knows where.

I run a hand over my face and focus on breathing. If I think about a breath in and a breath out, a breath in and a breath out, then I will force my body to stop spinning. Concentration can sometimes overcome those sensitive inner ear issues.

My stomach calms. The bay has stopped moving, for the most part. And another person looms over me.

Yash, her hair plastered to the side of her head by sweat.

"I'd say I'm never diving with you again, but that was *amazing*," she says.

I close my eyes. Hers is precisely the wrong reaction to a nearly disastrous dive.

"We're lucky," I say.

"No kidding," Yash says. "Do you realize what just happened?"

"Yeah," I say. "Orlando saved our lives."

Yash turns to him, grins, and says, "That's right. I almost forgot to say thank you."

He nods a little formally. "I'm sure you would have done the same."

I frown. If she's not talking about how close we came to death, and the joyful fact of our survival, then I have no idea what she's talking about.

"Boss," she says, putting her hands on my shoulders. "Do you know what's going on?"

"I know we're alive," I say. "That's about all I know at the moment."

"The runabout *disappeared*," she says.

"Yeah," I say, and then I realize she's not upset about that. The idea thrills her. "I assume you activated the *anacapa* drive."

"That's the thing," she says. "I didn't."

"How do you know?" Orlando asks.

She gives him a withering look, which is answer enough, I guess.

"If you didn't do it," I say, "who did?"

"The Fleet!" she says. "The Fleet retrieved it! They activated another *anacapa* and hooked into it. I'll wager it was targeted. They wanted *that* runabout and they pulled it out of the Boneyard."

I rub a hand over my face. I'm covered in sweat too, not because my suit's environmental system had failed, but because of the stress to my system out there, as I tried—yet again—to survive that damn runabout.

"I don't know how you know that," I say, and I'm rather surprised at how grumpy I sound.

"That's the only explanation," she says. "I'm sure the data will back it up."

I'm not. A million things could have pulled that runabout out of here. It might have had a distress signal going, and we activated that signal when we touched the navigation panel, which then got an ancient sector base to pull the runabout away. That scenario mirrored what happened to the *Ivoire*, and was probably more likely, given the part of space we were in.

But Yash is exhilarated, and I don't want to ruin that. Not right now. Still, I have to say one thing.

"We have no way to check the data," I say. "I'm sorry, but—"

"But we do," she says. "I brought the data back from the navigation panel."

That's right. Her device. I wonder if she checked to see if there was data on it, or if she's just indulging in wishful thinking.

"Plus, we have that control panel," she says.

"No," I say. "I had to let it go, remember."

"I do," she says. "Because I caught it and shoved it into my belt with everything else."

I don't recall her doing that, but I was more concerned with getting both of us out of that cockpit—out of that runabout—before we got blasted into some kind of existential purgatory.

"You got it?" I ask, managing to rise up on one elbow.

"Yeah," she says. "I have everything. And the runabout *activated*. The *anacapa worked*. Boss, this is the first indication we have, the first *real* indication that the Fleet still exists."

Orlando is watching me, as if he expects me to convince her otherwise.

Instead, I sit up all the way. I'm wiped out. Some of that is the loss of adrenaline as the adventure ends, but some of it comes from the fact that I really am not in the best physical shape. I probably shouldn't have gone on that dive after all.

Although, I'm not sure how good a rescue diver I would have been. I doubt I would have made it to the door of the runabout in record time, like Orlando had.

I'm not sure I could have rescued us. Or, rather, them. I might have been halfway along the line when that runabout vanished into foldspace or wherever the hell it went.

Then I let out a small breath.

"Mikk," I say. He doesn't respond. Of course, he doesn't respond. I'm not on comm.

"What is it?" Orlando asks.

"The probes," I say. "They're still inside the runabout."

"Oh, my God," Yash says. "We might be able to track them."

I can hear the hope in her voice. I inadvertently made her think that we can find the Fleet.

I'm not sure what we'll find at the end of this. I'm not sure if we'll find anything.

But I know we have a chance of tracking that runabout.

And it excites me, almost as much as it excites her.

27

I struggle to get to the bridge. My body's shaking, and I can barely walk. I've had new divers, tourist divers, react like this, but no one on this run has seen this reaction before.

"I need clear liquids, and something with sugar, salt," I say. "Get Jaylene to bring me something on the bridge. But water now."

Orlando leaves my side, moving faster than I expected. I don't know if Yash is with us. It takes too much effort to turn around.

But I continue to creak my way to the bridge. I need to get up there. I need to see what's happened.

Orlando comes back in what seems like an instant with water and some kind of juice. I drink the water, spilling some of it on my chin and down my already sweat-covered shirt. I'm a mess, and I don't care.

I can feel the euphoria of a good dive starting through me. Or maybe it's the euphoria of a near miss.

Orlando hands me a cool bottle of something clear, and I drink it as we get on the elevator. Yash joins us. Orlando hands her a bottle as well. She doesn't look like she needs it, though.

I expect my reaction is because of my already depleted reserves.

The elevator opens on bridge level, but not directly in the bridge. I like that about the *Sove*. Some of the older model Dignity Vessels make bridge access much too easy.

Or rather, I usually like it. I feel like I'm covering fifty kilometers instead of a few meters. Orlando has taken my elbow, which is quite a concession for both of us. I smile at him, though, letting him know it's all right.

The bridge doors slide open and we step inside.

Jaylene is already there, alongside Elaine. I had forgotten that I wanted Elaine on this mission. I'm glad she was there. She was probably the one who insisted Orlando leave when he did. Mikk sometimes errs on the side of continuing the dive.

Elaine wouldn't have done that in this circumstance.

I also realize it was her voice I heard on my comm, shouting "Boss" as I covered those last few meters to the bay door.

"Brief us," Yash says as she follows us inside.

I'm glad that she's taking over now. Mikk stands beside one of the panels, then sweeps a hand toward two holographic images. One of them has gone completely dark. All I can see is the shape.

He's going to make a presentation.

I ease myself into the nearest chair, limbs still shaking. Jaylene approaches me, puts a hand on my forehead, and takes the bottle from me. She sniffs it, then looks at Orlando.

"Water?" she asks.

He nods.

"I've got more in the other conference area, along with some broth and other liquids. Please get them."

I feel badly that he has to miss the beginning of this presentation. I swivel the seat toward it.

Jaylene pours the water on my head, and I sputter. It cools me down instantly.

I hadn't even realized I was hot.

"What the hell?" I said.

"You were overheating," she said, "and I knew I wasn't going to get you off the bridge or back in your full environmental suit. This will help. Now drink more."

Orlando hands me a glass. The man must have sprinted back and forth to the conference room.

"We done getting water all over my bridge?" Mikk asks, keeping his tone light to hide his concern. It's not working.

"Yes," I say, wiping my hand over my face. "Go ahead."

He taps one of the holographic models. It's one of the planning models we worked off of, with the *Sove*, the other Dignity Vessel, and the runabout highlighted.

"This is what this section of the Boneyard looked like before your dive," he says.

Then he touches the model that's dark. It comes to life, with only the *Sove* and the other Dignity Vessel highlighted. There's an actual gap where the runabout was.

"This is what this section of the Boneyard looks like now," he says.

"And in between?" Yash asks.

"Standard activation of an *anacapa* drive," he says. "The readings, everything, exactly what you would expect."

She frowns. Except for the layer of sweat, which is making her hair dry in spikes, she looks like the dive hasn't bothered her at all.

I used to be just like that.

I make myself drink some more. Jaylene is monitoring me, not paying any attention to the presentation.

"What about the ships around the runabout?" Yash asks.

"No impact that we can tell," Mikk says. "I have a lot of material, though, and we can study it."

"And no reaction from the Boneyard?" she asks.

"None," he says.

"What about before the runabout leaves?" she asks.

He frowns at her. "What do you mean?"

"That *anacapa* was activated remotely," she says. "How did that signal get inside the Boneyard."

My hair drips onto my shoulders. A rivulet of water runs down my back, making me shiver. Or at least, I think the water was what made me shiver.

It might have been Yash's point.

We can't get many signals in and out of the Boneyard. We've tried communicating through their force field, and it rarely works.

No wonder she's thrilled.

"We'll have to check," Mikk says. "I didn't see anything, but that doesn't mean anything. I was focused on you two."

I nod. "And the probes?"

His expression grows even more serious. "We don't have much. We have the lights coming on, some images of you, a bit of telemetry from the navigation panel as it starts up, and then…"

He looks at Yash.

She raises her chin, clearly bracing herself.

"I'm sorry," he says. "The images winked out. I can't re-establish contact."

"I expected that," she says. "I just figured we might be able to trace them."

"I can't," he says, "but you might be able to."

She nods. She runs a hand through her hair, leaving it even more spiky than it was. Then she rubs her hands on the back of her suit, forgetting that we haven't even taken time to change.

"Do me a favor," I say to Mikk. "Let me see exterior footage of the runabout from the moment we get inside until it vanishes."

"And I'll watch the energy signatures," Yash says, moving to one of the backup engineering panels. I would rather have her watch the visual footage with me, but I'm not going to argue right now.

I'm sure we'll be reviewing everything that happened today for weeks.

"All right," Mikk says. "Flat?"

"Yes," I say as Yash says, "No."

We glance at each other. Then she says, "Flat for now."

The screen in front of him springs to life, showing the section of the Boneyard that contains the *Sove*, the Dignity Vessel, the runabout, and a handful of other ships.

We watch. From this angle, there's no way to see the line we've run from the *Sove* to the runabout. There is no indication at all that anything is different about that runabout.

For several minutes, nothing happens. Then lights appear around the entire runabout. The lights flare on, and then they shut off. They do that three times before remaining on.

I don't remember seeing them, but I was rather focused on getting back to the *Sove*.

That bright light illuminates Orlando, who is a small speck on a barely visible black line. He reaches the main door. The images are too far away to show what he's doing there, but he's there for at least two minutes before Yash and I tumble out.

We look like small balls of dirt, rolling and falling and tumbling into the darkness.

Orlando dives after us, pulling on our tethers. I can no longer see the line from the *Sove* to the runabout.

I force myself to watch the runabout rather than the miniaturized version of the drama I just lived through.

The lights around the runabout grow even brighter. Then the entire runabout appears in sharp relief to something very dark—a hole, a blackness, *something*.

And then the runabout vanishes.

I don't see us any more either. Everything looks the same, except for the nanobits which, from this distance, look like they are moving in some kind of current.

It takes me a moment to understand what I'm seeing. There is a current of nanobits, pulling toward that blackness, before they veer away, as if they were barred from getting through it.

"Those nanobits," I say. "Are my eyes deceiving me or are there more of them?"

"More," Mikk says. "I saw that too, and already verified."

"So something in that interaction caused some kind of nanobit unbonding?" I turn toward Yash. "Is that something we have to worry about with the *Sove*?"

"We should check it out when we get back to Lost Souls," she says. "I'm wondering if that's a reaction unique to the Boneyard."

"I doubt it," I say, thinking of that very first Dignity Vessel we found, all those years ago, not to mention all the nanobits floating around Sector Base V when we arrived. "I've seen it before, and so have you."

She shrugs. Clearly, her focus isn't there, and I'm not going to push her, at least at the moment. Later, we can investigate all of this.

I have only one more question before I go clean up and rest.

"That *anacapa* drive," I say. "It clearly functioned. So our theory about the malfunctioning, dying *anacapa* drive was wrong."

"Elaine and I have already discussed that," Mikk says. "We're going to rerun some tests, now that the runabout is gone. We'll see what really is causing that energy burst that hurt the two of you."

I'm glad he didn't say *nearly killed the two of you*. I somehow don't want that thought in Elaine's head.

"There's no need to run those tests," Yash says. "We were right the first time."

Elaine makes a soft sound of disagreement. Mikk's lips thin.

"How is that possible?" I say. "We just saw the *anacapa* work."

"We saw remote activation of that *anacapa* drive," Yash says. "We didn't see it 'work.'"

"That's a distinction without much of a difference," I say.

"There's a lot of difference," she says. "Dead *anacapa* drives can't activate, but they have residual energy stored in what remains, energy that can't talk to other little bits of energy. A remote activation ignites the entire drive, brings in more energy than the drive needs, and unites those disparate bits of energy. If there's enough energy in the dead *anacapa* drive to move a ship, the remote activation will use it to propel the ship into foldspace. Once in foldspace, the other *anacapa*, the one that contacted the ship's *anacapa*, will be able to pull the incapacitated ship back to wherever it came from."

"Or wherever it's needed," Elaine says softly. It's not a question. Her eyes meet Yash's, though, almost in a challenge.

"Yes," Yash says. "Back to where it came from or to wherever it's needed."

"So," I say, "a small ship, like that runabout, would need less stored energy to get to foldspace than, say, the *Sove*."

"Exactly," Yash says. "There wasn't enough energy in that runabout's *anacapa* to move a ship one-eighth the size of the *Sove*. But that runabout is tiny. It took almost no energy at all to activate it, and get it into foldspace."

"You've seen this before," Mikk says.

"Not with small ships, but yes." Yash looks haunted. "I've seen it."

"With the *Ivoire*," I say.

"Our *anacapa* was in much better shape than the one in the runabout," she says, "but our *anacapa* was badly damaged. None of us could repair it. If you hadn't accidentally activated the *anacapa* in Sector Base V, we would have ended up like that corpse on that runabout."

No wonder she had looked at it for such a long moment. She hadn't been trying to figure out who that was. She had been thinking that, had circumstances gone differently, she and the entire crew of the *Ivoire* could have ended up like that.

I frown at the screen, rerunning the images in my head. I didn't see anything access that runabout, but then, whatever had done so might not have been in the visible spectrum, or it might not have shown up on the two-dimensional image that I preferred.

"Did you get any readings on that remote access?" I ask Mikk.

"Wasn't looking for it," he says. "I don't know what I would have been looking for."

"I know," Yash says. "I'd rather look for it all at Lost Souls. I can take my time, compile information, see what we find."

"Do we need more readings from the Boneyard?" I ask.

"Not right now," she says.

I nod, suddenly feeling very, very tired.

"Then," I say, "it's time to go home."

28

WE SPEND THE NEXT DAY cleaning up various details that we need before we leave the Boneyard. I also want to make certain that the Boneyard itself has no real reaction to the loss of the runabout.

I half expected the Boneyard to fire on that empty space or to note that we've been active and maybe attack the *Sove*. But none of that happens.

Everything here is as it was before—except for the fact that the runabout is gone.

The disappearance of the runabout has transformed Yash from a rather dour woman to a woman filled with joy. I don't think I've ever seen her like this, full of purpose, working hard, and smiling all of the time.

The other crew members from the *Ivoire* seem lighter as well. I don't want to disappoint them, but I'm not as convinced as they are that whatever took the runabout belonged to the Fleet.

Not that it matters. We have a lot of data to sift through before we come to any conclusions. We have the staff at Lost Souls to do a great job faster than we can do it here.

We have other reasons for returning. Most important is, of course, Elaine. She needs better medical care than we can give her here. And Jaylene says I do as well.

I think she's being overly dramatic, but I will undergo any test that the various medical professionals want me to go through. I need to rebuild my strength. My reaction to this last dive caught me off guard.

But not necessarily in a bad way. Because the upside for me is this: I managed a dive while weakened in extremely difficult circumstances, and I survived it.

For a while, I thought I might have to give up diving.

I now know I won't have to at all.

I promised Jaylene I would rest before we leave, and I am, staring through the portal in my cabin at the Dignity Vessel we had been unable to dive.

I make that vessel a silent promise. We will be back for it.

I will be back for it.

Because, no matter how excited the *Ivoire* crew is by our discoveries, those discoveries mean less to me than the discoveries still lurking in the Boneyard itself. Answers to great mysteries. Historical data beyond my wildest imagination.

And technology that—even though it's from the past—is well beyond anything my people or the people in this sector have come up with.

We'll go back, sift through the data, and see what we can learn.

But I'm returning to the Boneyard as soon as I can.

I have ships to dive.

And I can't wait to see what adventures they hold.

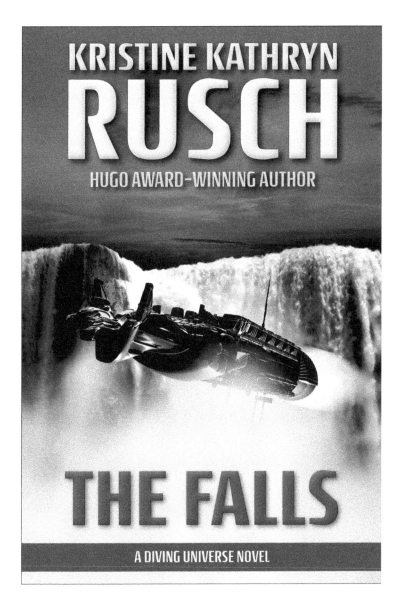

KRISTINE KATHRYN
RUSCH
HUGO AWARD-WINNING AUTHOR

THE FALLS
A DIVING UNIVERSE NOVEL

Learn more about the Runabout and the history of the
Fleet in *The Falls: A Diving Universe Novel*.

On Sale Now.

Turn the page for a preview.

1

THE SHOES STARTLED HIM. Rajivk Agwu stopped at the edge of the black path and stared at them. Two pairs, both brown, smallish and well-worn, were neatly lined up against the black wall. Just beyond them, the water of Fiskett Falls churned, blue and gold and gray. A slight rainbow formed on the edge of the spray as the late afternoon sunlight hit the water just right.

Usually, Rajivk never stopped at this overlook. It was halfway up the Falls, and provided a view mostly of the water as it cascaded into Rockwell Pool below. A lot of people liked to study the water as it fell. It was dramatic and gorgeous and always powerful.

But this overlook was damp and cold, with very little light. It had been built by some of the first engineers to arrive in the Sandoveil Valley, hundreds of years ago. They were entranced with Fiskett Falls, just like everyone else who visited this remote part of Nindowne, and because the engineers were from the Fleet, they decided to make it easy and safe to view the Falls.

They built several overlooks, using the same nanobits that they would use to carve Sector Base E-2 several miles from here. The overlooks were solid, if a bit too slippery. The nanobits were designed to build underground caverns that could withstand thousands of years of constant activity. So they could handle the elements, even the elements as they were on the far part of Ynchinga, the tenth—and least populated—continent on Nindowne.

The weather was always active here. Twelve seasons, although most of the people who lived in Sandoveil, still using Earth Standard thousands of years after the Fleet had left their home world, liked to say they had four seasons—the Earth equivalent of fall, winter, spring, and summer.

Really, though, this part of Ynchinga had predictable variations: early-fall, mid-fall, late-fall—and the same for the other seasons.

It was mid-fall right now, the kind of day that made Rajivk grateful, because he knew the next few seasons would be stormy and difficult. The cool sunlight that created the lovely rainbow at the edge of the mist would become rare in the next week or two. Late-fall always brought rain- and ice-storms, sometimes so severe that the only way Rajivk could get to work would be to take the underground transports, which he hated.

It made him feel like he was on the *Qoraxda* again, unable to feel any wind on his face or smell rain in the air. He had been born in the Fleet, always traveling through space, rarely spending any time planetside, but he was not born *to* the Fleet.

The day that the *Qoraxda* came to Sector Base E-2 for the once-every-five-years overhaul was the day that changed his life.

This was another day that would change his life—or so most of the employees of the sector base had said. He hadn't believed it, because he thought the change a minor one. Although the news must have had some kind of impact on him because he had decided, at the spur of the moment, to take the upper trails around the Falls on his walk home. The upper trails added an hour to his walk. An hour and just a bit of treachery.

Viewed from a half mile away, the Falls looked symmetrical, the water evenly proportioned across its entire plunge to the pool below. Up close, it became clear that the looks were deceiving. The center of Fiskett Falls poured the most water below, and the edges were thin and clear.

The edges froze in late-fall or early-winter, making the Falls even narrower, and much more dangerous. All of the moving water squeezed into the middle section, shutting down the lower overlooks.

This overlook was always closed from the beginning of the freeze until mid-spring, but most of the locals stopped using this overlook in late-summer.

That was why the shoes startled him. They didn't look like tourist shoes. These shoes were nearly boots. He could tell just from a glance that the shoes had local modifications. It took some particularly strange footwear to climb the paths. The nanobits were too smooth, and impossible to reconfigure, so local footware designers modified boots generally used in zero-g. The boots would cling to surfaces, but not too much. They would adjust according to the conditions—if the path was wet, the boots would provide a different kind of traction than if the path was covered with a thin sheet of ice.

If locals decided to wear shoes like these, they still had the modifications. And these shoes did.

Then Rajivk shook his head. Shoes shouldn't have startled him, no matter how unusual they were. Maybe some hiker had set them here to wait for a return. Although they were getting wet.

And climbing up the trail in mid-fall could be dangerous. Those thin sheets of ice were invisible to the naked eye. Many a hiker tried to take the upper paths around the Falls, only to slip and break a limb. Some of the local guides only took tourists up the paths if the tourists wore basic environmental suits, the kind that space tourists had to use to prevent easy injury.

Rajivk walked the upper paths as much as he could, and hadn't worn an environmental suit up them ever. Once he moved here, fifteen years ago, he made it a point to learn everything he could about Fiskett Falls and its trails.

And the first thing he learned—the thing he reminded himself about every single spring—was that the Falls were dangerous. They could kill if he didn't pay attention every single second.

That was probably why he shouldn't have come up here today. He was distracted. For the first time since he started working at the sector base, everyone had been required to attend a meeting. Usually information got recorded and shared, or trickled down through departments.

The announcement made at the early morning meeting was simple enough: the base had finally received its closure date. Thirty years from right now, the base would shut its doors. It would stop taking Fleet ships for their every-five-years maintenance twenty years or so from now, depending on the rotations. And it would stop taking emergency repairs at least two years before closure.

Closure itself would take every moment of those two years. It would be better, the administrators said, if the base had five years to shut down operations. Everything had to be done perfectly, and no one wanted to leave some Fleet ship stranded, too far from Sector Base F-2 to have its *anacapa* drive make easy contact with the base's drive.

In theory, a Fleet ship could contact *any* existing sector base, anywhere, so long as the Fleet ship was in foldspace. In practice, the contacts became difficult once a ship moved several sectors away from a base.

The Fleet learned, over the years, to move the bases, along with the ships, mostly as a precaution.

Rajivk believed in precautions when it came to space. He was raised on Fleet ships, born in motion, as they liked to say, and he had chosen to stay at Sector Base E-2 even though everyone knew it would be the next base closed. The Fleet kept only three sector bases open at one time—at least for ship repairs. In addition, there was always one base (sometimes two) under construction at the far end of the Fleet's trajectory, and there was often (although not always) one base in the process of shutting down at the back of the trajectory.

Rajivk wasn't even born when Sector Base D-2 had shut down. As long as he had been alive, Sector Base E-2 was slated to close. The only difference today brought was an actual date—and that date was so far in the future, a good third of the crew would already be retired.

He ran a hand through his hair. The spray from the Falls had beaded on it. The sunshine and the warm(ish) mid-fall weather had kept him from noticing the growing damp. The spray wasn't really spray today, more like a fine mist. It smelled faintly of sulphur—the entire Falls did sometimes—and fresh air with just a hint of the decay that signaled mid-fall was nearly over.

Seasons changed. They moved forward, just like the Fleet did. The change of seasons was as reliable as the fact that the Fleet would eventually leave a sector. At some point, the Fleet would be gone forever. And then it would become a memory, at least in this part of this galaxy. Then it would become a rumor or a legend or a myth—or, as some said, forgotten completely.

Although the Fleet would leave, much of its tech would remain on this little corner of Ynchinga, and eventually, the people who lived here in the Sandoveil Valley would remember that some group had initially colonized this area, but they wouldn't remember who.

The rainbow was slowly disappearing. The sun was moving along the horizon. He needed to move too if he wanted to get home before dark.

But first, he walked over to the shoes. He had to investigate them. They bothered him. Anything out of the ordinary bothered him up here.

Annoyingly, his boots stuck to the path. The black nanobits weren't wet enough to make the first level of the boots' tech effective, but they were wet enough to activate that first level.

Another reason he rarely walked to this overlook.

His heart started pounding as he approached the shoes. He observed his own reaction as if he were outside himself. Sometimes the proximity to the Falls made his heart race. The roar of the water, the damp and cold air, the constant and hard vibration all around him sometimes grabbed control of his limbic system.

Rajivk wasn't sure if his increased heart rate was because of the Falls or because of the shoes. He couldn't see the shoes' owners anywhere. Leaving two pair of shoes behind, deliberately, was either symbolic or really stupid.

Apparently, part of him was worried that he was dealing with really stupid. Had two people taken off their shoes, climbed onto the smooth wall to see the water better, and fallen?

If so, he might find them on the other side of the wall, unable to get purchase to climb back up it. He knew of some kids who had fallen off this part of the overlook, but they were local kids. They knew that they couldn't climb back up. They threaded their way along the pointed rocks, moving slowly, and making sure of every step until they made it to the other side of the overlook, and crawled the last few feet to the path itself.

Of course, they had the proper shoes, and they had even brought hiking gear, so they had the right kind of gloves and rope and all kinds of tech that enabled them to survive the most treacherous part of their fall.

And none of them had been hurt.

His mouth was dry. He had been breathing through it, nervously. He didn't want to find someone on the other side, clinging to those rocks.

He braced his hands on the cool wall. Water had beaded on the top. He actually dislodged puddles that he hadn't been able to see. He wondered if this part of the wall was ever dry.

He leaned forward. He would have shouted, but it would have been impossible to hear his voice over the thunder of the Falls. He looked down, saw slick wet rocks the color of slate. Tiny runnels of water threaded down the sides of the rocks, as if creating their own miniature waterfalls.

He hadn't expected it to be so wet and violent on that side of the wall. He had known about the kids, had thought that they had landed on a dry patch, but of course they hadn't.

There was no dry patch on that side of the wall. Technically, there was no dry patch on this side of the wall.

Clearly luck—and fantastic equipment—had allowed those kids to grip the rocks at all. Sheer determination that enabled them to crawl away from the water. And even more luck that got them past the overlook, to the drier rocks on the side, before they finally reached the path he had walked up.

Whoever owned the shoes on the overlook beside him hadn't had the proper equipment. Shoes were good on the path, but to handle the wet side of the Falls would require full-fledged boots, maybe some kind of suit, and climbing gear.

Maybe the shoes owners' had removed the shoes and put on boots. But he saw no evidence of that.

And why would someone do it? There were people who tried to best the Falls, and some who succeeded, but that took more than good boots and a willingness to step into a wall of water, free-falling at the rate of thousands of cubic feet per second. Rajivk had never wanted to try. It seemed like certain death to him.

Rajivk wiped the water from his face. He couldn't even see into that wall of water. He didn't understand the attraction.

He glanced at those shoes, so neatly lined up, and felt a surge of anger. Maybe someone had left them to taunt him. Maybe they were supposed to signify something he didn't understand.

Whatever the reason, he hadn't asked to be the one to find them. He hadn't asked to worry about them.

And, he finally decided, the shoes were not his concern.

He backed away from them, and then when he reached the path—and only then—did he shake the water off his shirt and pants. If he had known he was going to get that close to the Falls, he would have worn his outdoor gear.

But he'd been thinking about the sector base's end date, the fact that he could envision his choices again—if he wanted to take them. He could stay here for the rest of his life, knowing he would retire in thirty years whether he wanted to or not. Or he could apply to work at one of the other sector bases. Or he could stay here, find some other job, and move even farther away from the Fleet.

Those thoughts were why he had chosen this upper path. Because he knew, deep down, that if he wanted to continue his career into the future, he would have to move.

He would have to leave the Falls.

And he couldn't imagine leaving the Falls.

Just like he couldn't imagine climbing into them.

He sighed.

He would have to do something about those shoes, and unfortunately, he would have to do it soon.

2

A DOOR SLAMMED TO HER RIGHT. Bristol Iannazzi raised her head from the diagnostics screen. She had been deep in the repair of an *anacapa* drive, the kind that required firm concentration or she would send the entire room into foldspace. Or something worse. She didn't like to imagine worst-case scenarios, not when it came to *anacapa* drives.

She stood in the middle of her lab, a deeply secure room in Sector Base E-2 on Nindowne. The base was miles beneath the surface near the city of Sandoveil. She'd been thinking about their location all day, weirdly enough, even though she shouldn't have been.

She probably shouldn't have been working on the drive, either, not after the morning's meeting. The entire staff of the sector base had to show up at the beginning of the morning shift—even third-shift workers who really wanted to go home and get some sleep.

They met in the amphitheater on the ground level, a space rarely used. It had smelled musty, which she had deemed appropriate once the administrators had made the announcement.

Sector Base E-2 would be closing thirty years from now. The date was set. By that day, all functions of the base would cease. The new base, Sector Base G-2, would have been running at full capacity for five years by then, and would take over Sector Base E-2's place in the rotation.

All the work that they had to do, all of it, from this moment forward, would be with the closure in mind.

She had known the closure was coming. Everyone did. They were informed in their yearly job review, and reminded that they could request a transfer to Sector Bases F-2 or G-2 at any point, and that transfer would most likely be approved.

The problem was that this base had existed for more than three hundred years, and entire families had built their lives around it. Iannazzis had worked at Sector Base E-2 for five generations, with a sixth in training. Bristol's daughter had just gotten a job here last year, and her granddaughter—all of ten—talked of nothing more than working in the base.

Which was closing.

The other two active bases weren't even in this sector. They were light years from here, in wildly dissimilar places, chosen by some Fleet engineers to meet some standard that Bristol didn't care about.

She, at least, had imagined life off Nindowne, but so many who worked here couldn't conceive of it. She had warned her daughter about the upcoming changes, and her daughter had scoffed.

Mom, they've been saying the base would close for years. It's not going to happen in our lifetime.

Well, it was now.

Bristol ran a hand through her short-cropped hair and set down the tiny screwdriver she'd been using. The light at the tip shut off as she set it down. She closed the casing around the *anacapa* drive, then put the drive in a specially built storage unit, to protect herself and the room.

She really wasn't concentrating enough to work on the *anacapa*. If she kept thinking about the base closure instead of the delicate work she'd been doing, she truly would be a danger to herself and others.

Her lab was one of two dozen such secure labs, built under layers and layers of rock, deep in the Payyer Mountain range. The walls were smooth and black, constructed by the same nanobits that made the spaceships used by the Fleet.

In theory, the thick black walls would hold in any explosion and protect the mountains themselves from catastrophe. Such theories had been tested in other sector bases, not this one, and Bristol was deeply aware that each sector base was different.

There had never been a catastrophic accident at Sector Base E-2, and if their luck held for another thirty years, there would never be one.

The room had no windows, although some of the walls had clear screens over their surface. The screens would activate if someone outside the room wanted her to see something important or if one of the major and unexpected DV-class ships arrived into the sector base. At that point, the ship's *anacapa* drive and the base's *anacapa* drive would activate at least one screen in every room on the base, so that the crew was notified of the ship's arrival.

Walk through the wrong area when a ship arrived, and you could die, horribly.

The screens rarely activated, though. She preferred to use the holographic screens on her equipment or little screens she could attach to her work area. There were shelves everywhere, and more tools than almost any other workroom.

Bristol liked using the best tool for the job, and sometimes the best tool was obscure.

Since she was one of the most experienced *anacapa* engineers in Sector Base E-2, she felt safest working alone. Besides, if she ended up making a mistake—and everyone did, no matter how good they were—then she wanted to make sure the only person who died in the blast was her, and not anyone else.

Which was why the sound of a door slamming bothered her. The door to her right wasn't an exterior door. It was a blast door, separating this room from the ship storage area. She wasn't working on a DV-class ship. She was working on an FS-Prime runabout from the *Ijo*, which had arrived for its five-year upgrade one week ago.

She had graduated from DV-class ships, under direct supervision, to handling the smaller vessels connected with the ships years ago. But she hadn't worked on anything like the runabout before.

It was an older technology, one that the Fleet now recommended be retired. Captains of the DV-class ships didn't have to listen to recommendations, however. They could maintain older equipment as long as they felt it useful.

She hated the runabout. The FS-Prime designation referred to fold-space. The geniuses in ship design way back when hadn't wanted to call these runabouts *Anacapa* models, so they hid it with the FS designation.

This model was the only runabout model with an *anacapa* drive. For most of its history, the Fleet did not put *anacapa* drives in ships smaller than a DV-class vessel. Then, those geniuses, working before she was born, decided to test runabouts with *anacapa* drives. Early in her career, those drives had been the bane of her existence.

But she, and several other engineers, had convinced most captains in the Fleet to retire their FS-Prime runabouts. Only a handful of captains had held out, including Captain Harriet Virji of the *Ijo*.

No surprise that this ancient runabout was malfunctioning. The problem was, of course, the *anacapa*, which was smaller than the average *anacapa* drive. The small size was also a hindrance, because it carried a lot of power, but didn't have some of the redundant controls.

Anacapa drives sent ships into foldspace. If the drive was used properly, it would send a ship into foldspace for a short period of time, and then the ship would return to the same coordinates in regular space. Ships could also use foldspace to travel across sectors, using beacons that the Fleet had set up in various sectors.

Sector Base E-2 had *anacapa* beacons, and could pull ships in trouble from anywhere in three nearby sectors—and maybe even farther away than that. No one had really tested the reach of the beacons.

But everyone knew of stories in which beacons malfunctioned at long distances. That was one of the reasons the base was going to close.

The Fleet had moved beyond this section of space, heading forward as it always did. In theory, by the time that Sector Base E-2 closed, there would be no more Fleet vessels within easy activation range. They would be better served by other sector bases, and that travel through foldspace would be safer.

She was always cautious when she spoke about foldspace. Not only had she never traveled in it, she didn't entirely understand it. No one in the Fleet did, and that made everyone who worked on the *anacapa* drives nervous.

Some of the captains believed that foldspace was a different part of the universe. They believed the *anacapa* drive actually folded space, allowed the ship to travel across that fold, and end up elsewhere. They cited the fact that the star maps were drastically different in foldspace, so different that they were completely unrecognizable.

But the theorists who studied foldspace believed that foldspace itself might be another dimension, something they didn't entirely understand. Some other theorists believed the foldspace was a different point in time—some*when* else, not some*where* else.

And a few of the theorists believed that the *anacapa* sent the ship into an alternate reality, and then, somehow—magically, Bristol thought— brought the ship back again.

She didn't even have a guess. She had been trained on the *anacapa* drives, so she understood what the interior of a drive should look like. She understood how to test it in the lab to make sure the drive was functioning properly.

But if she or her family were to ever be invited to travel via *anacapa* drive, she would respectfully refuse. She didn't like the fact that the drive could send her somewhere else, in a way that no one entirely understood. She knew, because she studied it, that ships got lost in foldspace all the time, and that terrified her even more.

The fact that she wouldn't go through foldspace was one of many reasons why she would never work at another sector base. To get to those bases, she would have to take a DV-class ship that traveled through foldspace. She would have to experience a working *anacapa* drive from the inside of a ship.

She wasn't willing to do that, which was rather hard to explain, since she worked on *anacapa* drives every day.

She sighed softly. Maybe she hadn't heard the door. Maybe she had misinterpreted another sound.

Or maybe she had been so deep in her work that she hadn't noticed someone else walking through her workspace.

That idea made her shudder.

She waved on one of the larger screens. She recorded her work from three angles. She recorded it from above, taking in the entire room, so she could see if she took the wrong tool for a particular job. She recorded it from the top of the *anacapa* drive so she could see what her fingers were actually doing. And she recorded it from the tools themselves, making a record of her every move.

The caution had saved her from catastrophic mistakes more than she liked to think about. Sometimes, viewing her work on the three separate recordings at the beginning of the following day made her revisit what she had already done. If she had started up from where she had left off, she would have probably destroyed the device or blown herself up.

Or blown herself—and the room, and part of the base—into some part of foldspace. Somehow. Somewhere. Or some*when*.

The idea compounded her off-kilter feeling. She had been this way all day. It was unusual enough to have an all-base meeting; the fact that it had started at the beginning of her workday had thrown off her routines, making her feel behind from the moment she set foot into the room.

Alone.

"Overview of the entire room, please," she said to the screen. She had set the voice command to respond to her voice only. Anyone else would have to use the access panel beneath the screen. But she liked accessing her work from here. "Show me the last hour at the usual pace."

The usual pace was a pretty fast scan. Her eye was good: she could see mistakes in her work at speeds where most people saw a blur. It felt intuitive when she worked like that, even though she knew it wasn't. She processed things quickly; she just couldn't always articulate what she saw.

This time, though, nothing caught her attention—until she thought she saw a movement at the door to the right.

She noted the time stamp, and let the replay continue all the way to the current moment. She saw nothing else unusual.

"Replay at one-half the usual speed," she said, and then gave a time stamp for the start five minutes before the stamp that she noted.

She watched again, and sure enough, the door to the right bowed open slightly, and then banged shut.

"Normal speed from the same point," she said. "With sound."

She usually had the sound off because she had learned, years ago, that when she concentrated deeply, she either hummed a tune or she talked to herself. She found neither trait attractive. In fact, she found them massively annoying.

But she wasn't going to look or listen to herself this time. She was going to watch, in real time.

She moved the holoscreen kitty-corner so that she could watch the door in real time while watching the replay. The fact that she moved the screen made her realize that she was deeply unnerved. She hadn't allowed herself to feel that before.

She turned down the sound on the replay. The door opened silently. And she heard nothing except the room noise, not even a hum from her, until the door slammed closed.

The sound, turned low, still made her jump. Her pulse pounded, and her mouth was suddenly dry.

She had a couple of choices. She could leave the room, then report this. Or she could continue to work as if nothing happened. She could check out the room herself. Or she could ask for security.

Only she didn't dare ask for security out loud. She would have to do it on some kind of private setting, on a screen.

She had never done that before. But she knew she couldn't work in here any longer. Even if she wanted to concentrate, she couldn't—not with enough focus to work on an *anacapa* drive.

If she left, then whoever it was (*what*ever it was) could escape.

If she stayed, then she might be in danger, although she wasn't sure what kind of danger.

Although she didn't want to think about what could be behind that door, something not human that had forced it open.

Because the runabout had a feature she hated: to remove and check the old *anacapa* drive, she had to replace it with a different *anacapa* drive. The runabout couldn't even sit idle without one. It would begin its emergency procedures alerts without a drive.

That was one reason the FS-Prime class of runabouts was no longer being made. They were delicate in a strange and unusual way, mostly about their equipment. And ships in space couldn't be delicate in any way.

Her skin crawled. What if the *anacapa* she had placed inside the runabout as a temporary measure was causing some kind of problem? What if what was going on in that room had no human agent at all?

Her heart beat even harder.

If that were the case, she needed to leave.

But she couldn't think of anything an *anacapa* could do that would cause a door to open and slam shut like that.

Except activate.

She backed away from the blast door. Then she went to one of the platforms, and stared at the controls for a moment. She could hit the emergency beacon, but that might start an alarm, warning everyone to leave the area.

And if an *anacapa* had been deployed, that would be important.

But she didn't know, and she didn't want to investigate on her own.

Because if someone were in that room with the runabout, then she had just given that person warning.

And who knew what that person would do to her?

She certainly didn't.

She keyed in a request for an immediate security presence, saying she couldn't tell anyone the nature of the emergency.

And, with a last-minute thought, she also asked for the security detail to arrive in environmental suits.

Then she signed off, and grabbed her suit from the container she kept it in. The suit looked dusty and a tad too small.

But she was going to squeeze into it.

She *had* to squeeze into it.

Because she had no idea what was behind that door.

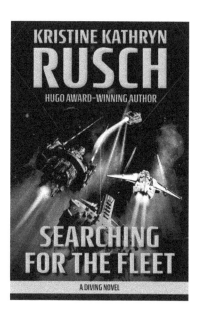

The next Diving novel—launches fall 2018

Be the first to know!

Just sign up for the Kristine Kathryn Rusch newsletter, and keep up with the latest news, releases and so much more—even the occasional giveaway.

To sign up, go to kristinekathrynrusch.com.

But wait! There's more. Sign up for the WMG Publishing newsletter, too, and get the latest news and releases from all of the WMG authors and lines, including Kristine Grayson, Kris Nelscott, Dean Wesley Smith, *Fiction River: An Original Anthology Magazine,* *Smith's Monthly,* and so much more.

Just go to wmgpublishing.com and click on Newsletter.

ABOUT THE AUTHOR

New York Times bestselling author Kristine Kathryn Rusch writes in almost every genre. Generally, she uses her real name (Rusch) for most of her writing. Under that name, she publishes bestselling science fiction and fantasy, award-winning mysteries, acclaimed mainstream fiction, controversial nonfiction, and the occasional romance. Her novels have made bestseller lists around the world and her short fiction has appeared in eighteen best of the year collections. She has won more than twenty-five awards for her fiction, including the Hugo, *Le Prix Imaginales,* the *Asimov's* Readers Choice award, and the *Ellery Queen Mystery Magazine* Readers Choice Award.

To keep up with everything she does, go to kriswrites.com. To track her many pen names and series, see their individual websites (krisnelscott. com, kristinegrayson.com, retrievalartist.com, divingintothewreck.com, fictionriver.com). She lives and occasionally sleeps in Oregon.

CPSIA information can be obtained
at www.ICGtesting.com
Printed in the USA
LVHW031533120419
613988LV00001B/193